& Ally

The Big Storm

Norm Feuti

HARPER
alley

An Imprint of HarperCollins Publishers

For Mom

One

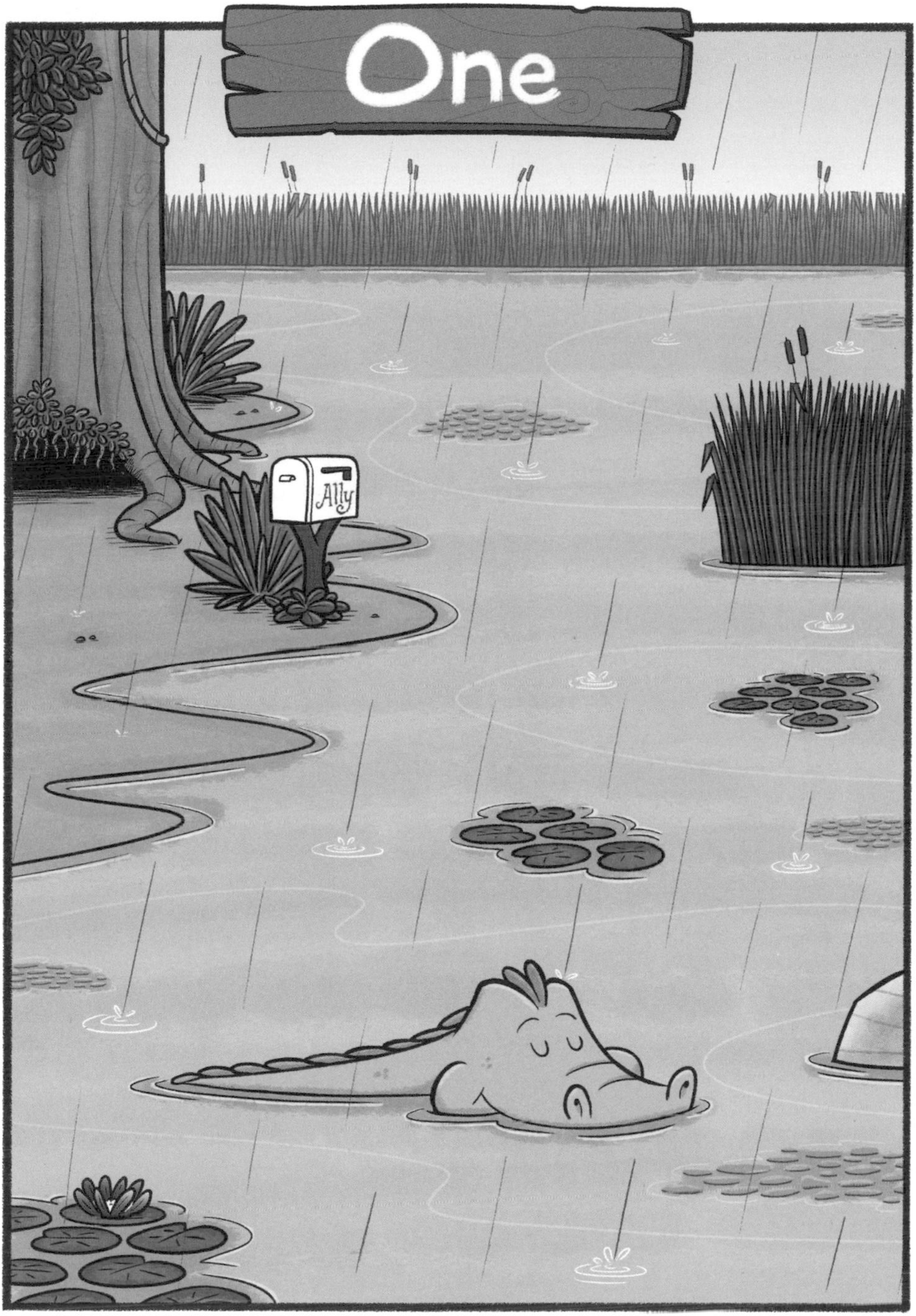
Ally

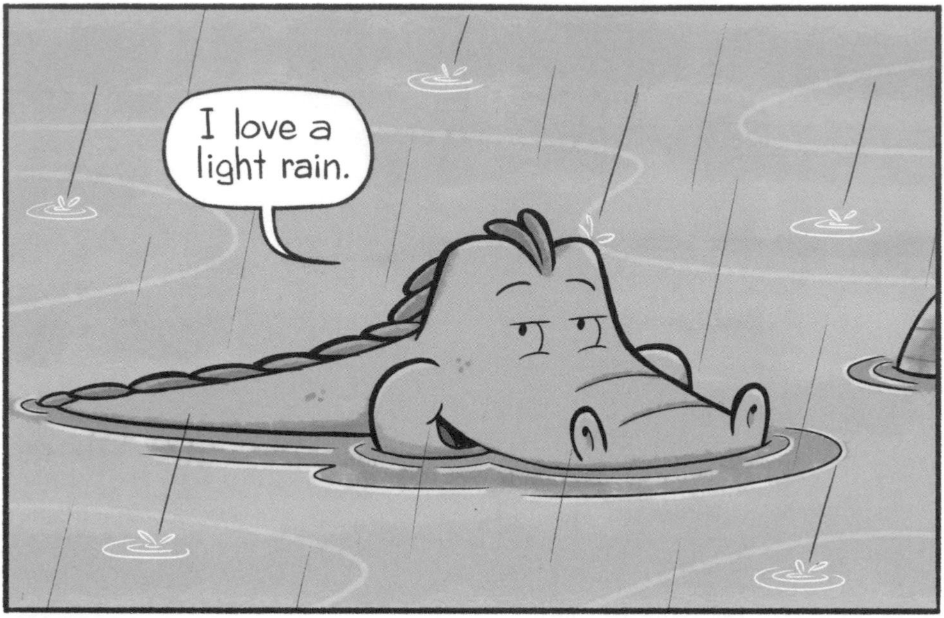
I love a light rain.

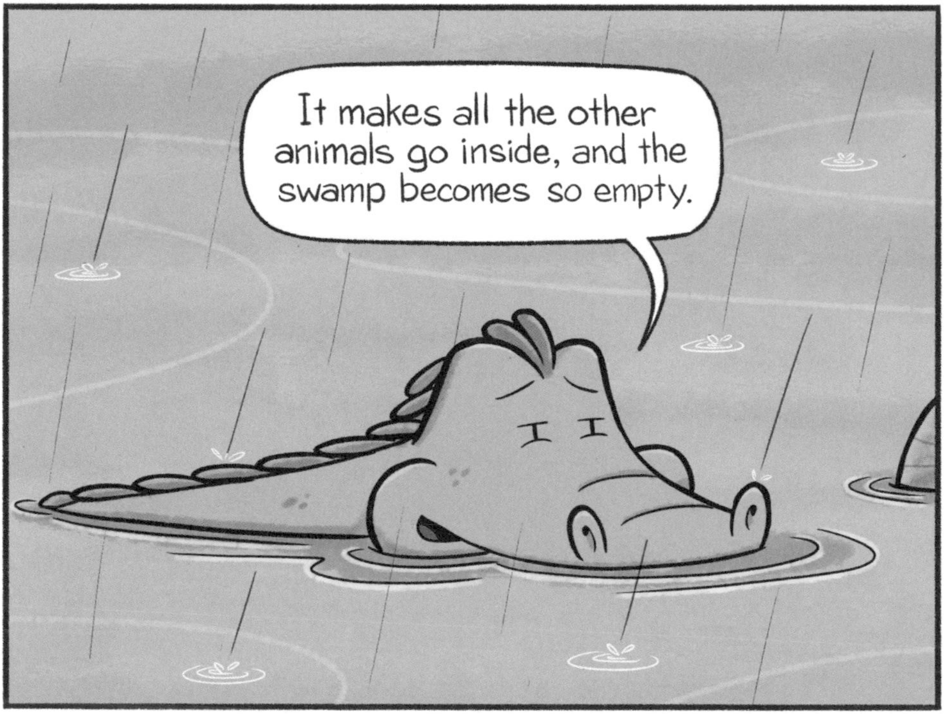
It makes all the other animals go inside, and the swamp becomes so empty.

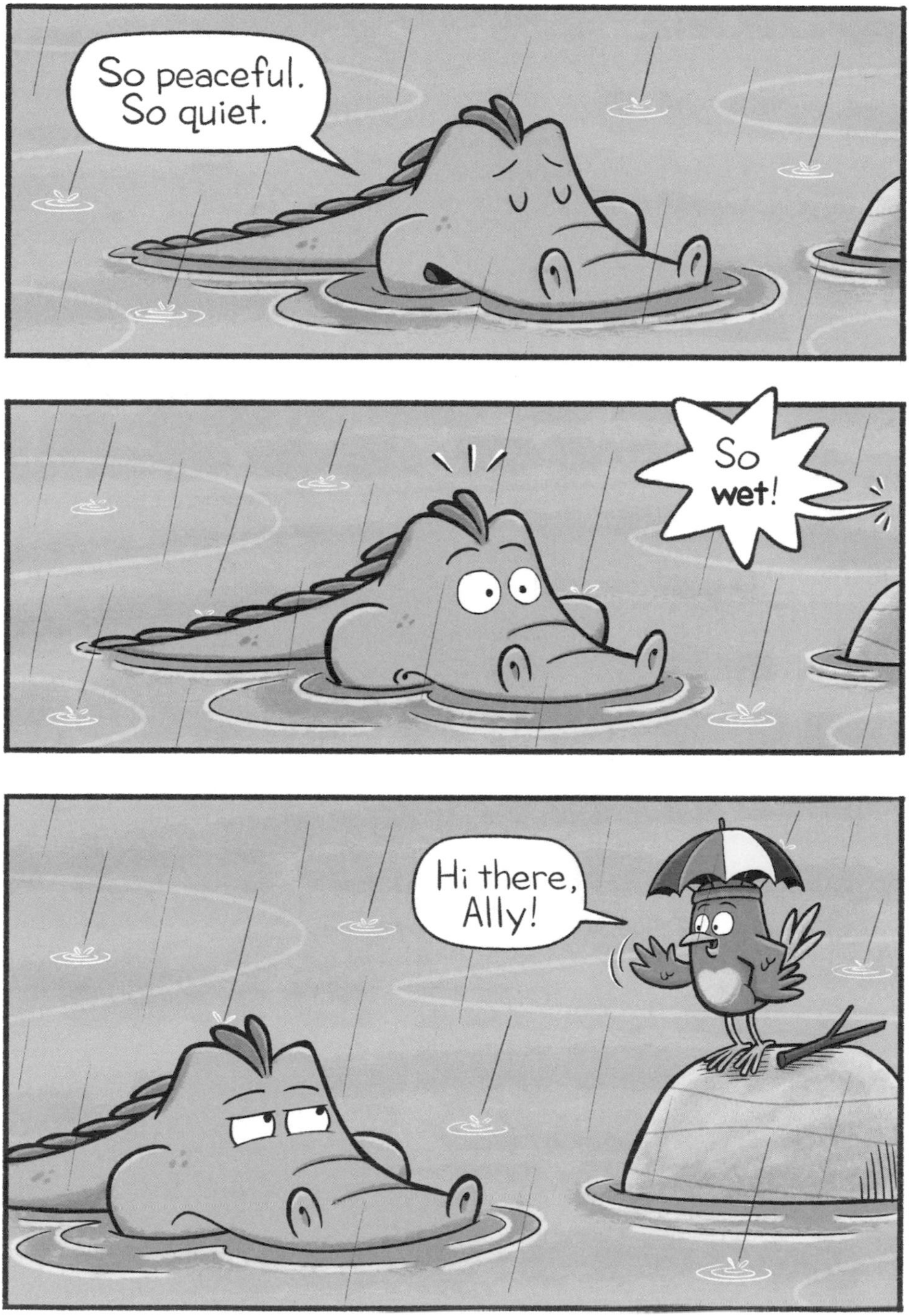
So peaceful.
So quiet.
So
wet!
Hi there,
Ally!

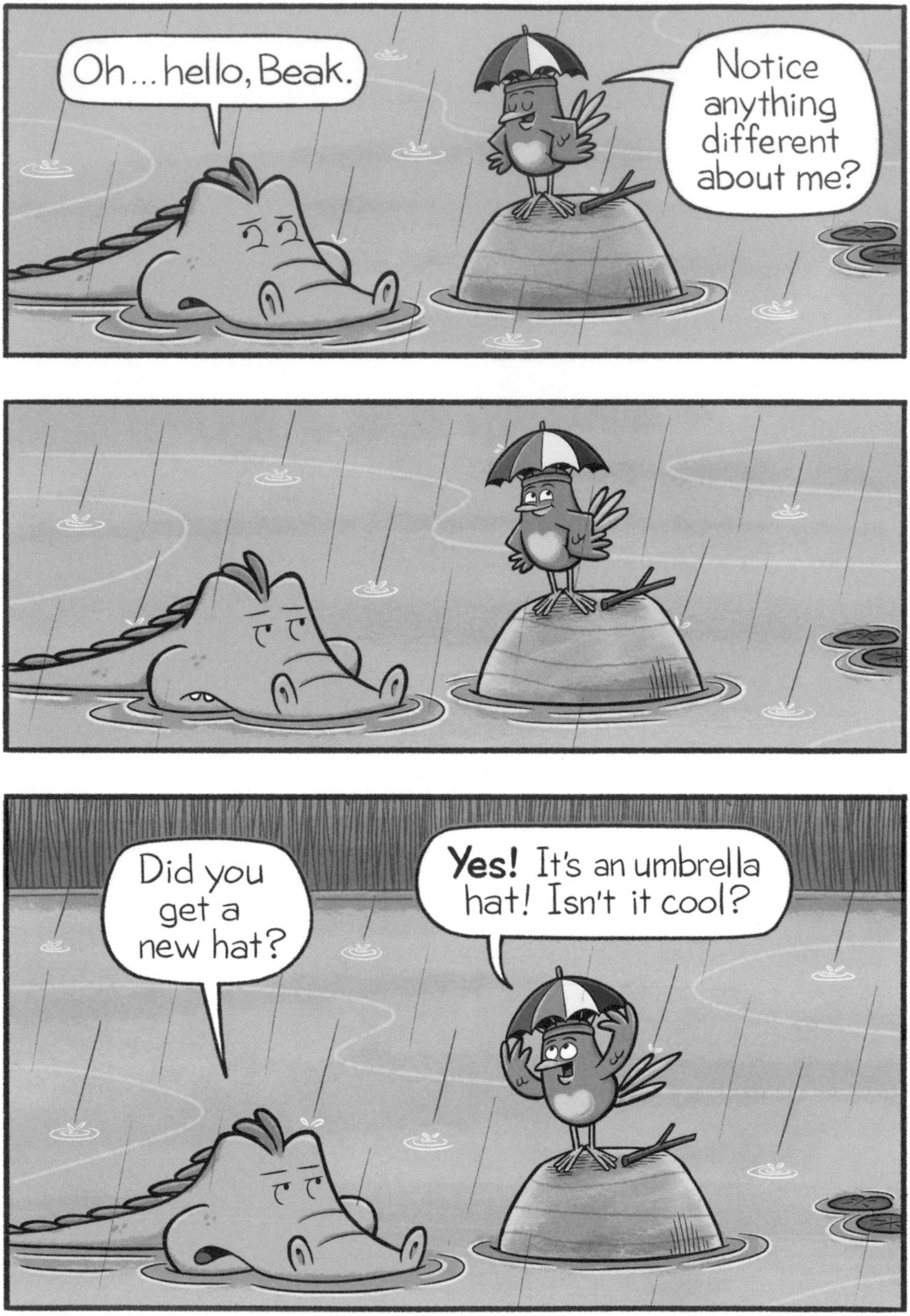
Oh... hello, Beak.
Notice anything different about me?
Did you get a new hat?
Yes! It's an umbrella hat! Isn't it cool?

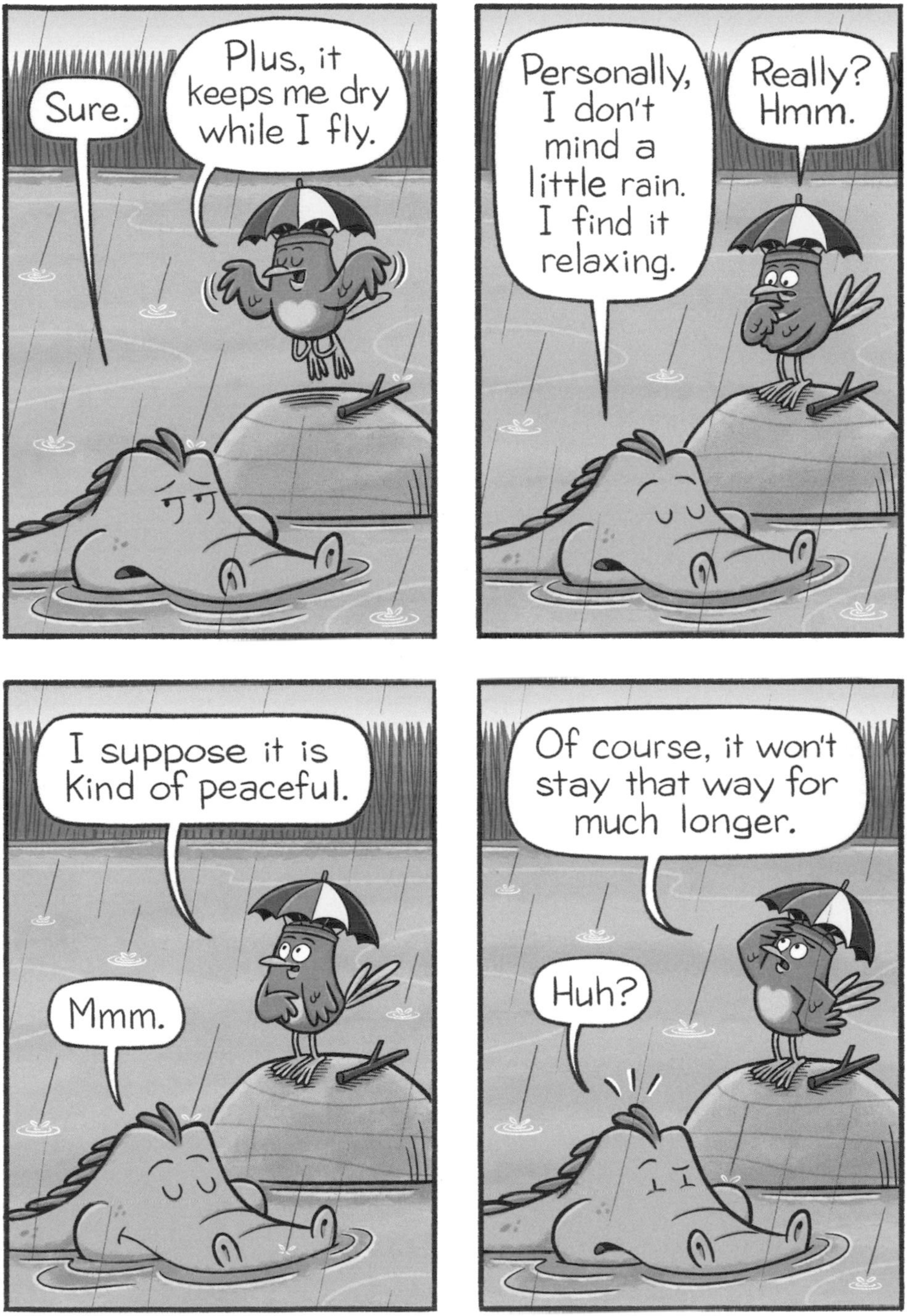
Sure.
Plus, it keeps me dry while I fly.
Personally, I don't mind a little rain. I find it relaxing.
Really? Hmm.
I suppose it is kind of peaceful.
Mmm.
Of course, it won't stay that way for much longer.
Huh?

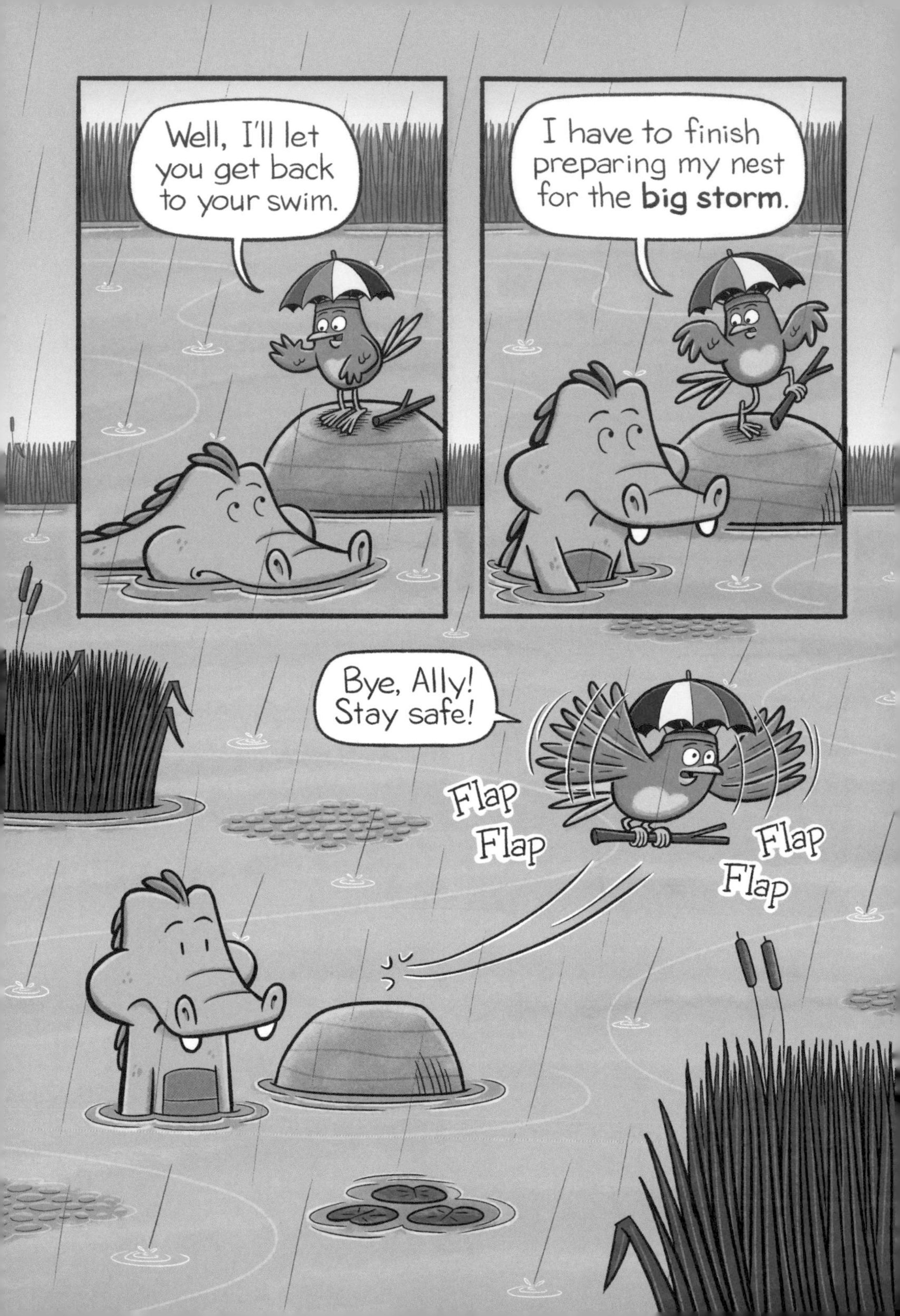

Well, I'll let you get back to your swim.
I have to finish preparing my nest for the **big storm**.
Bye, Ally! Stay safe!
Flap
Flap
Flap
Flap

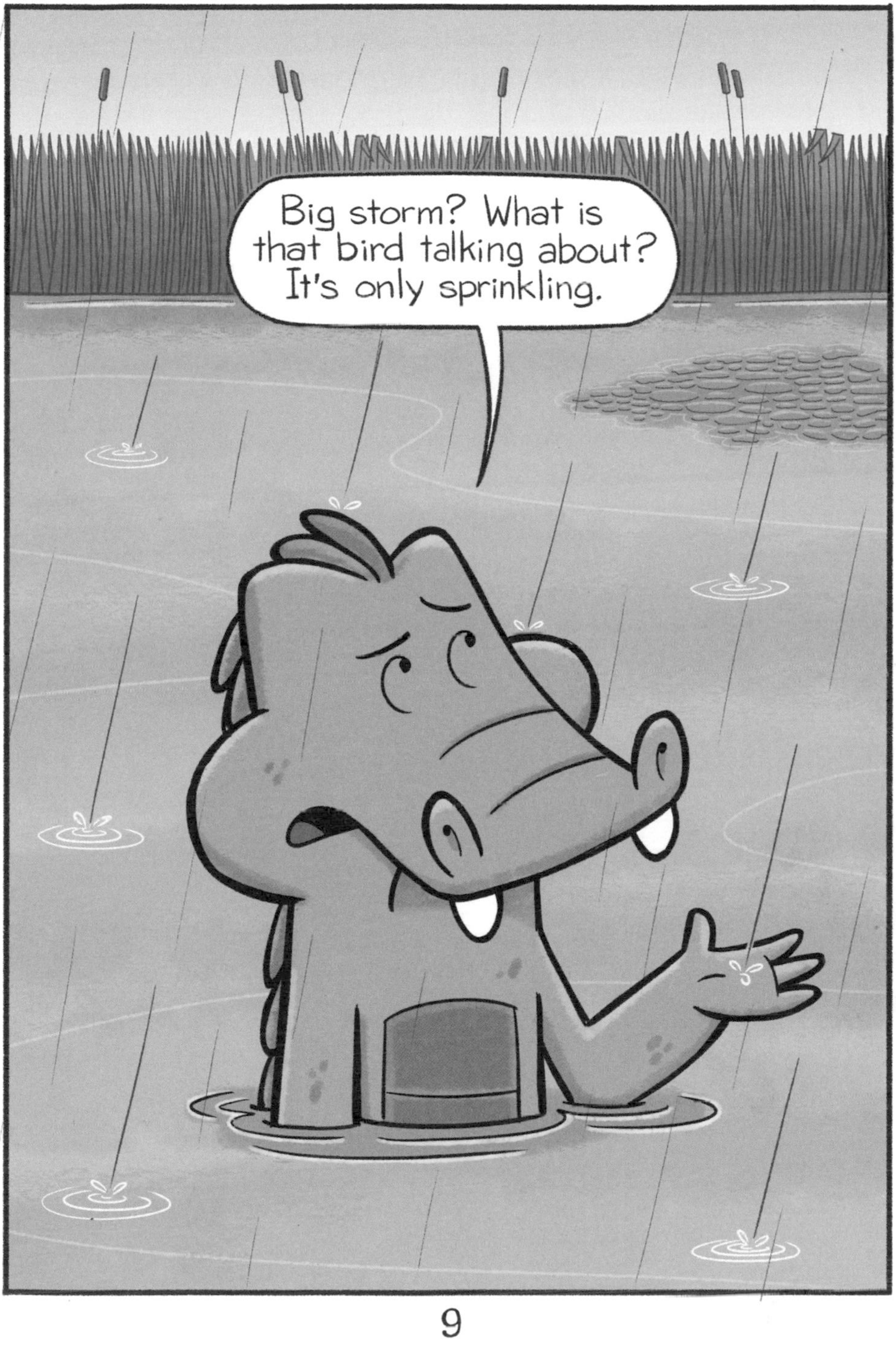
Big storm? What is that bird talking about? It's only sprinkling.

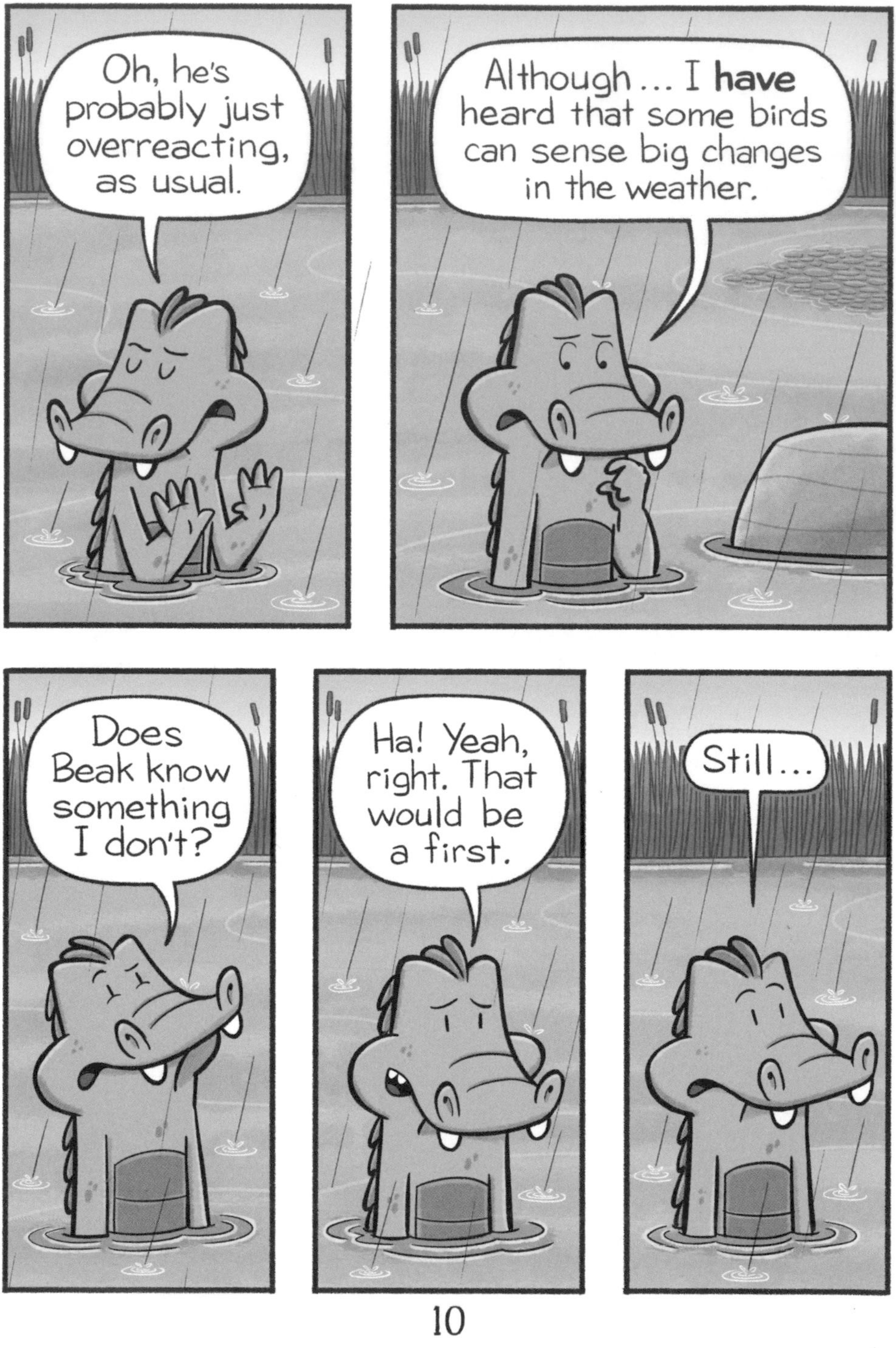
Oh, he's probably just overreacting, as usual.
Although ... I **have** heard that some birds can sense big changes in the weather.
Does Beak know something I don't?
Ha! Yeah, right. That would be a first.
Still ...

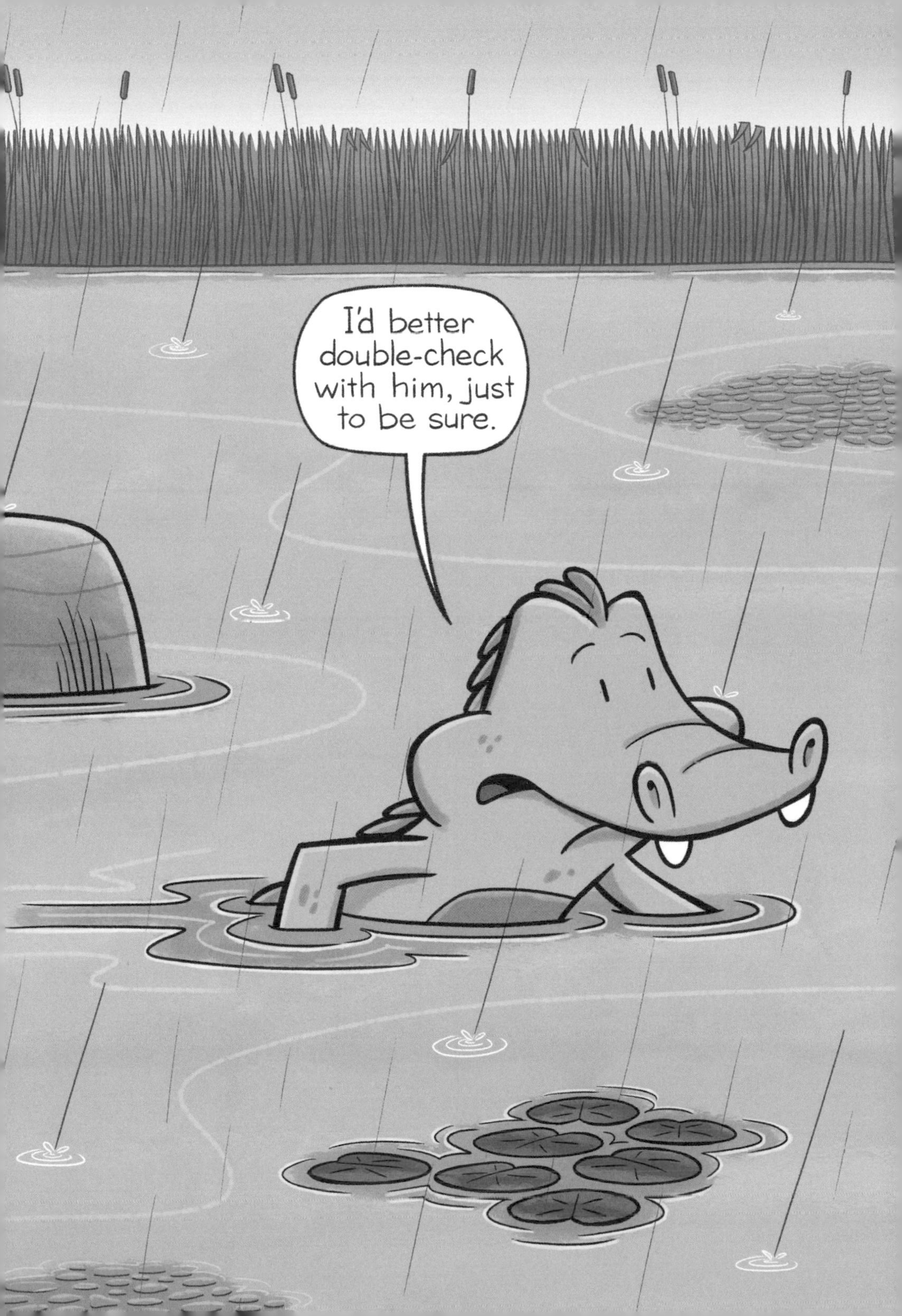
I'd better double-check with him, just to be sure.

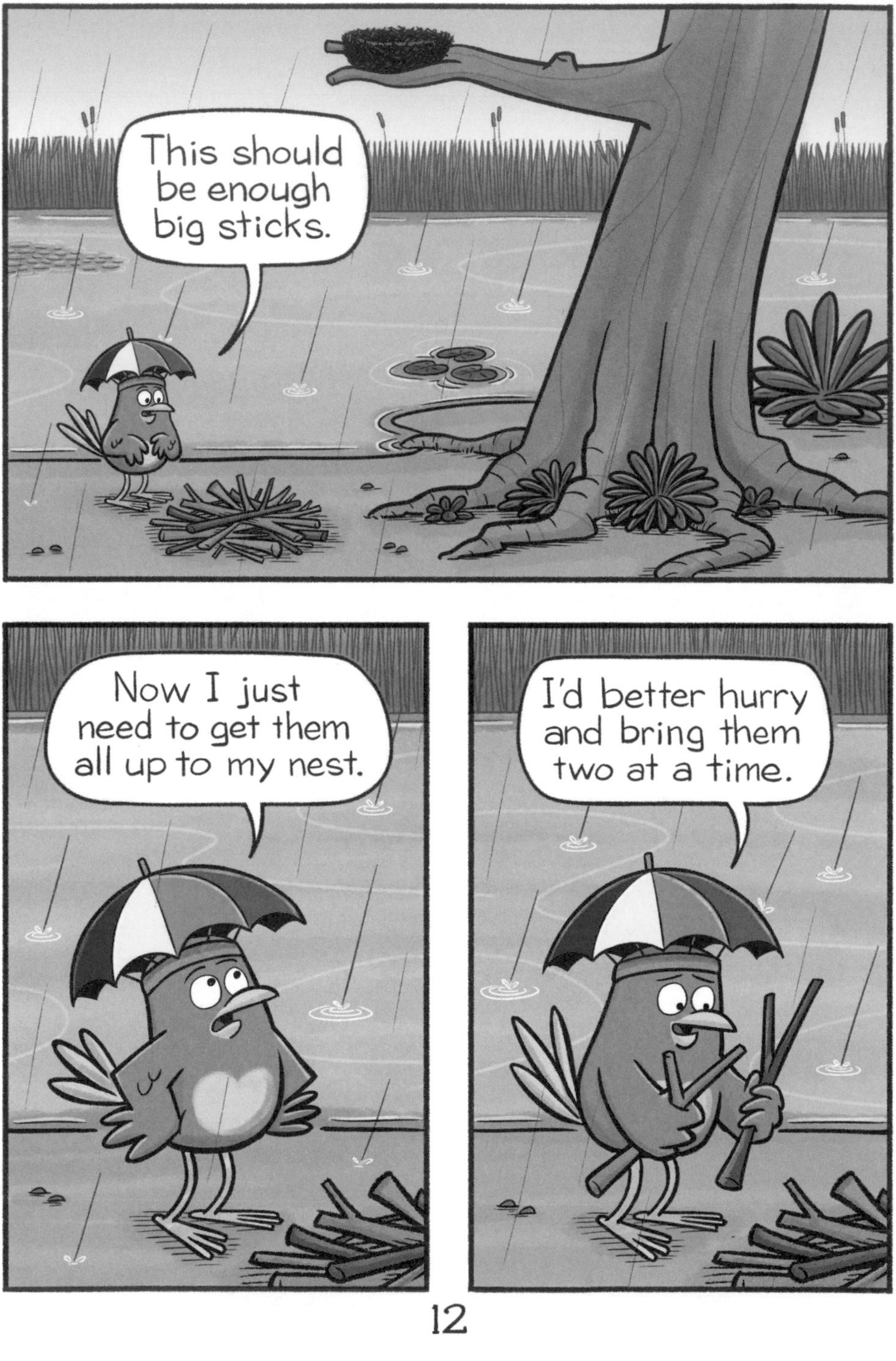
This should be enough big sticks.
Now I just need to get them all up to my nest.
I'd better hurry and bring them two at a time.

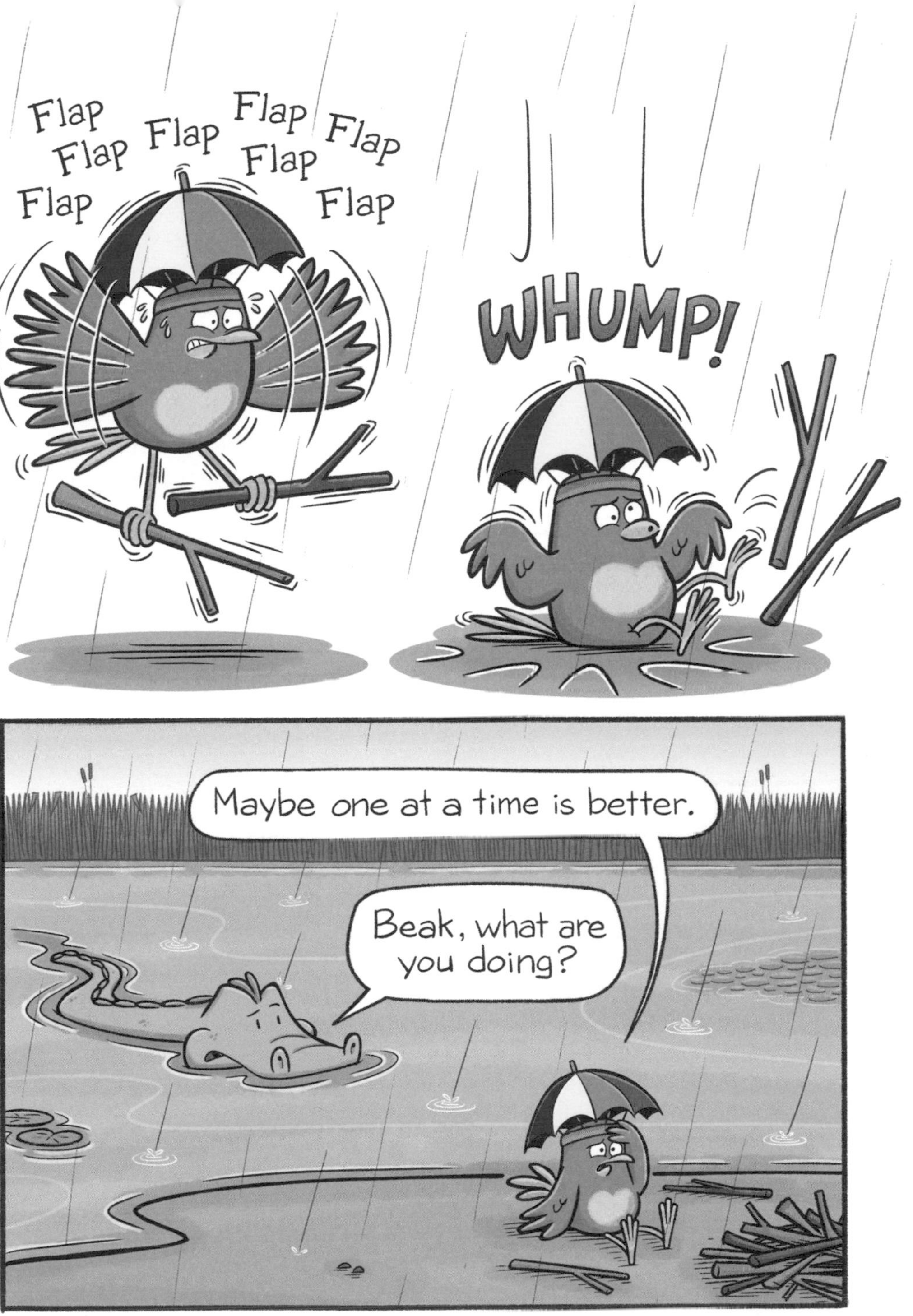
Flap
Flap
Flap
Flap
Flap
Flap
Flap
Flap
WHUMP!
Maybe one at a time is better.
Beak, what are you doing?

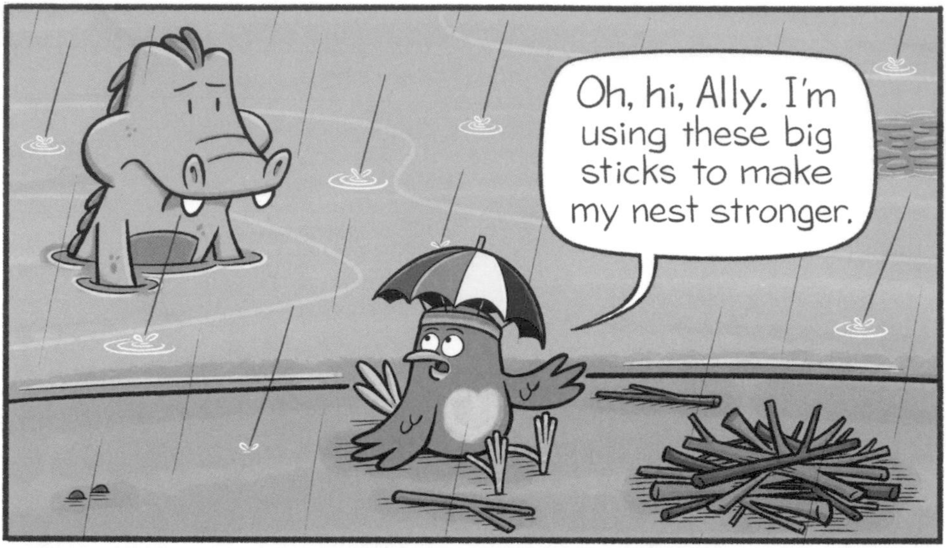
Oh, hi, Ally. I'm using these big sticks to make my nest stronger.

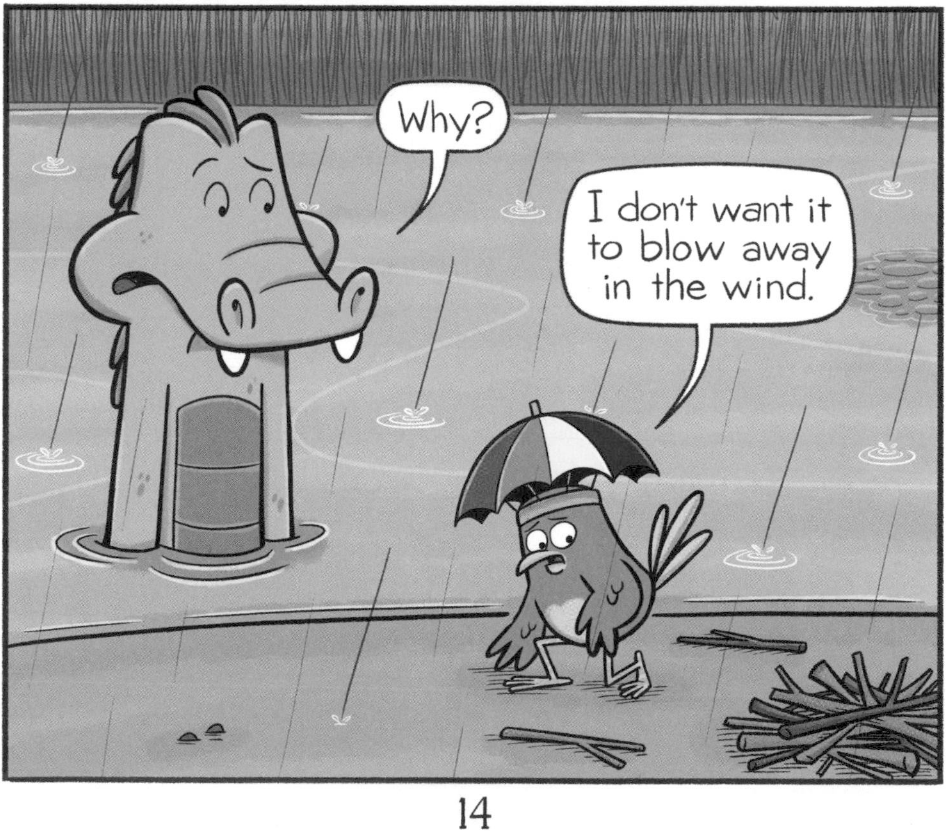
Why?
I don't want it to blow away in the wind.

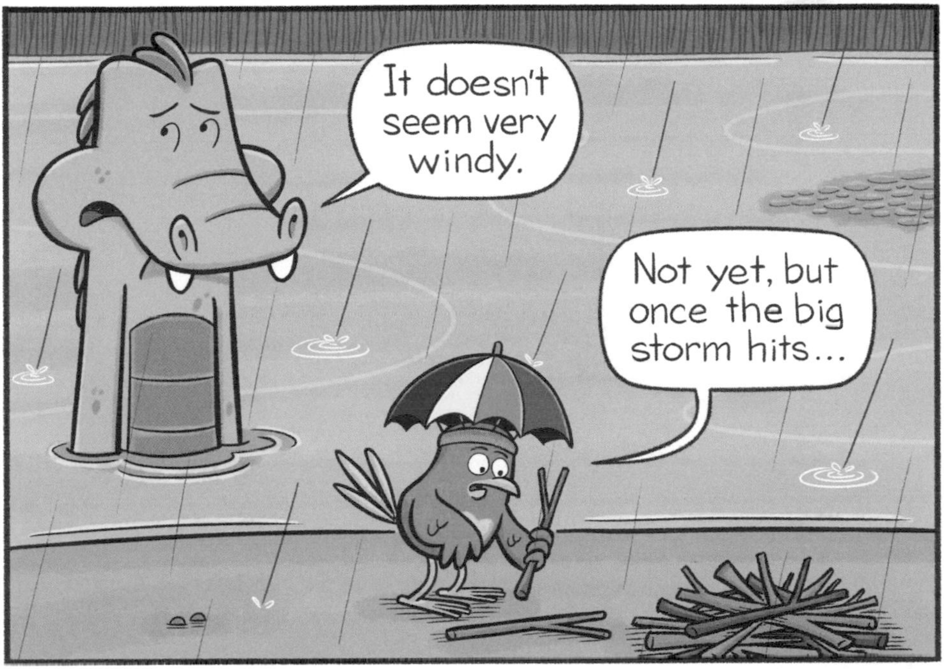
It doesn't seem very windy.
Not yet, but once the big storm hits...

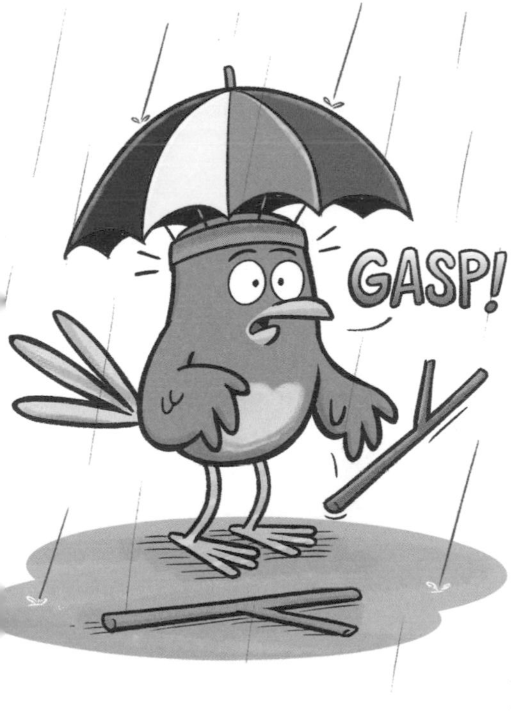
GASP!

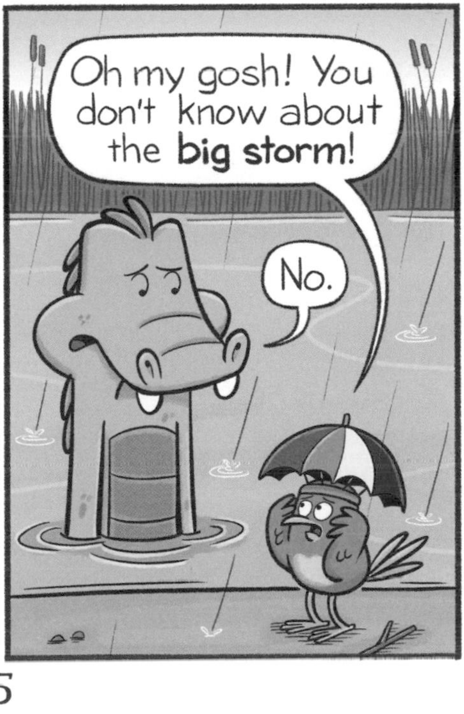
Oh my gosh! You don't know about the **big storm**!
No.

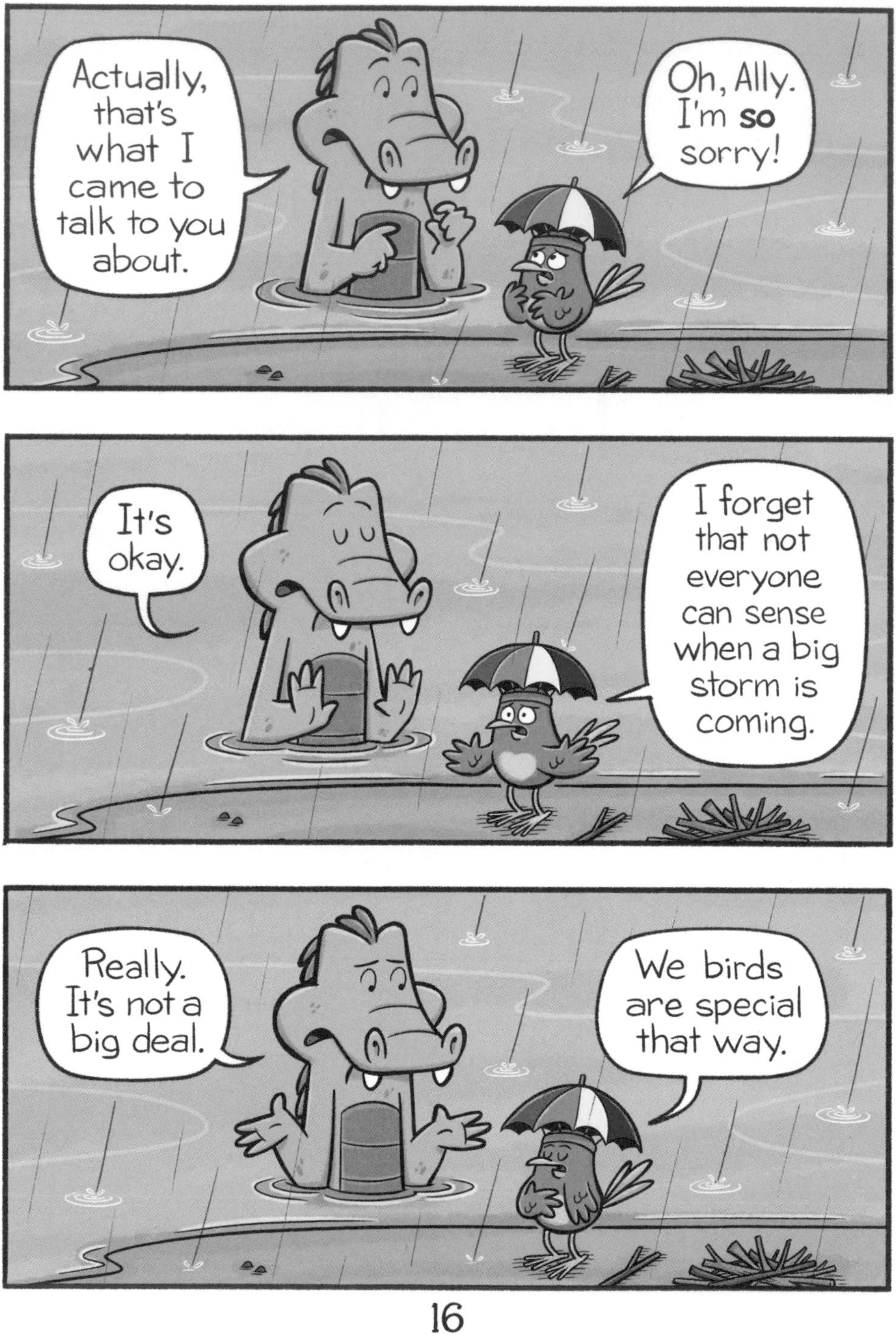
Actually, that's what I came to talk to you about.
Oh, Ally. I'm **so** sorry!
It's okay.
I forget that not everyone can sense when a big storm is coming.
Really. It's not a big deal.
We birds are special that way.

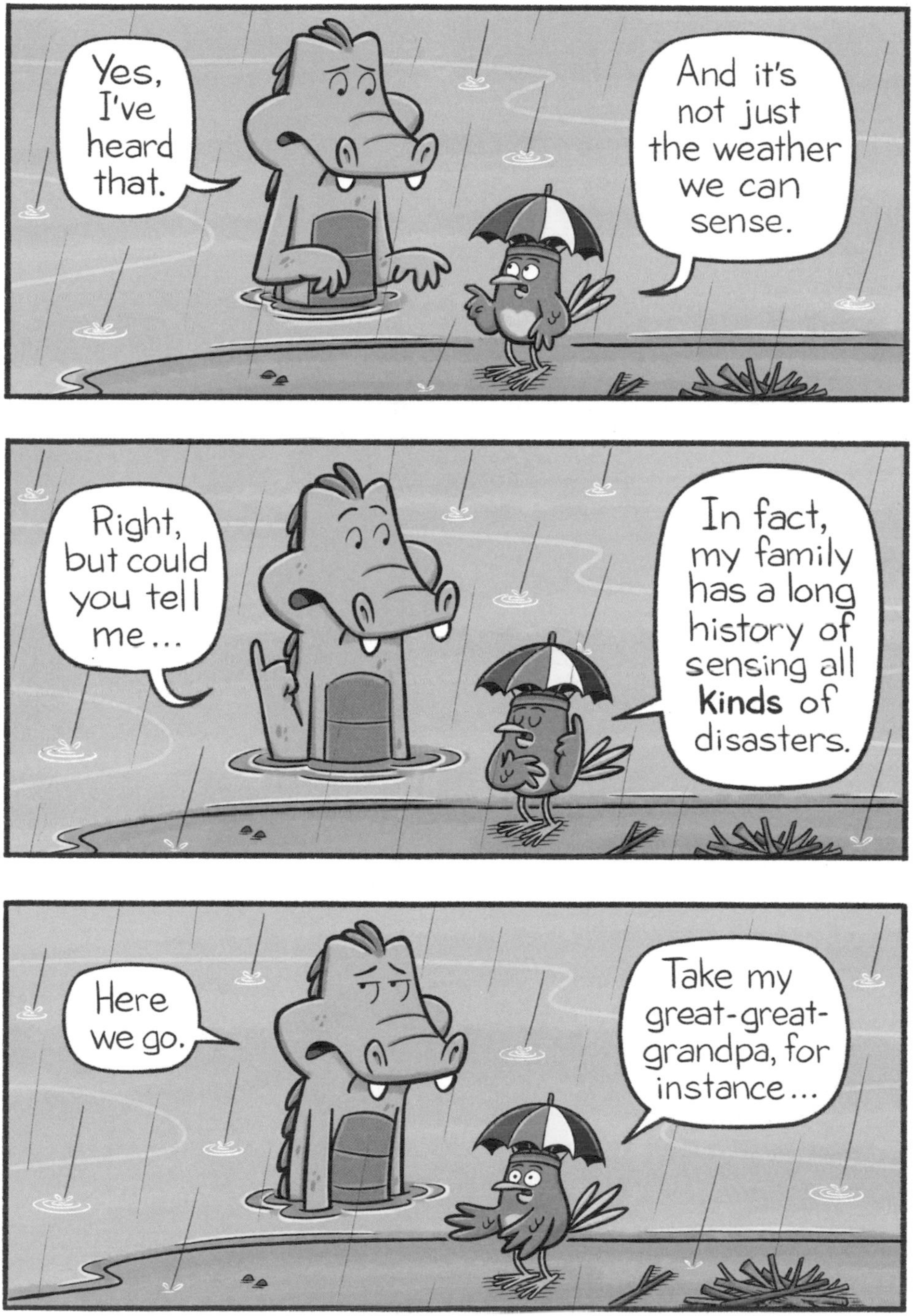
Yes, I've heard that.
And it's not just the weather we can sense.
Right, but could you tell me...
In fact, my family has a long history of sensing all **kinds** of disasters.
Here we go.
Take my great-great-grandpa, for instance...

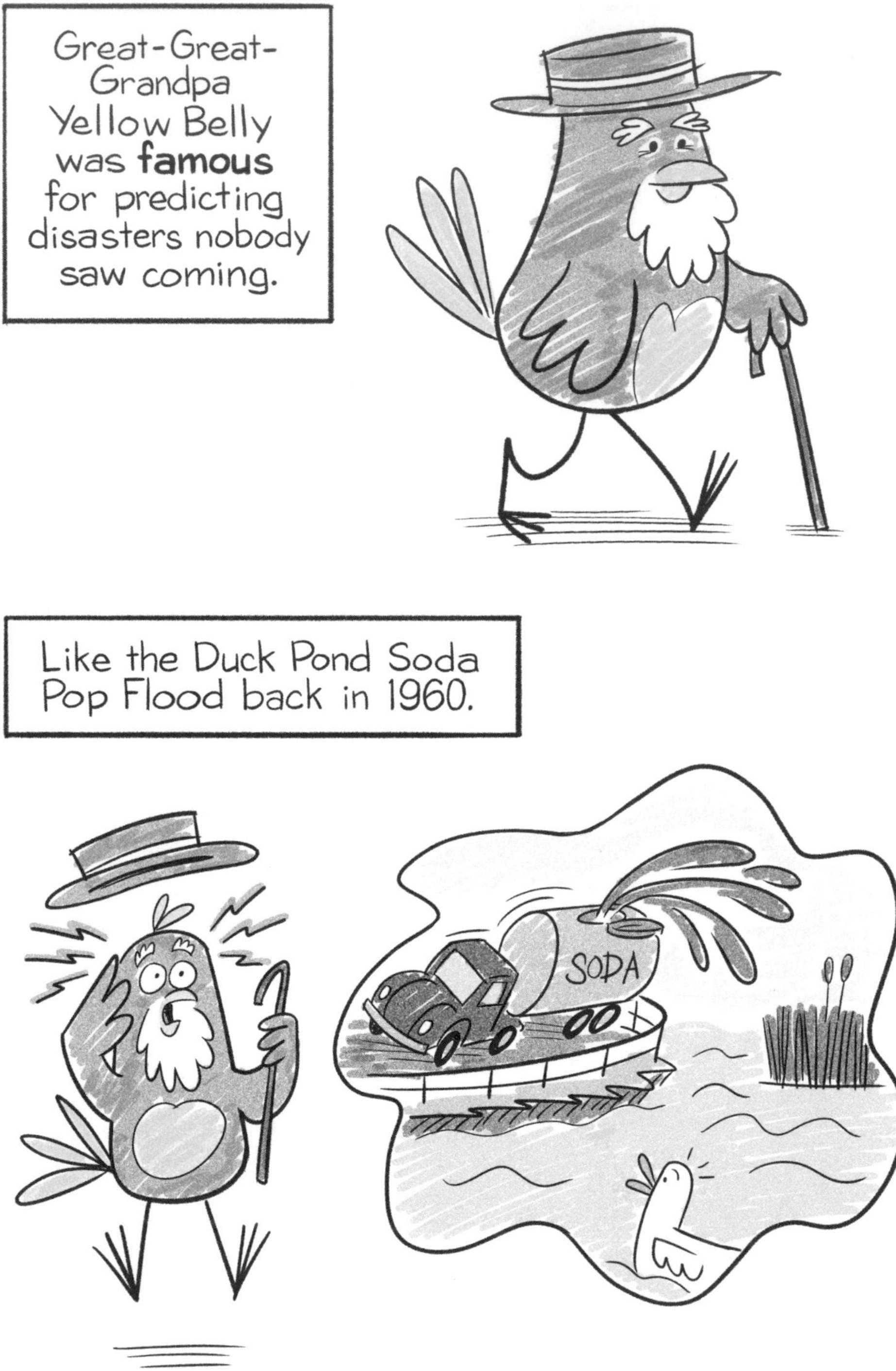
Great-Great-Grandpa Yellow Belly was **famous** for predicting disasters nobody saw coming.
Like the Duck Pond Soda Pop Flood back in 1960.
SODA

And the big Ostrich Earthquake back in 1973.

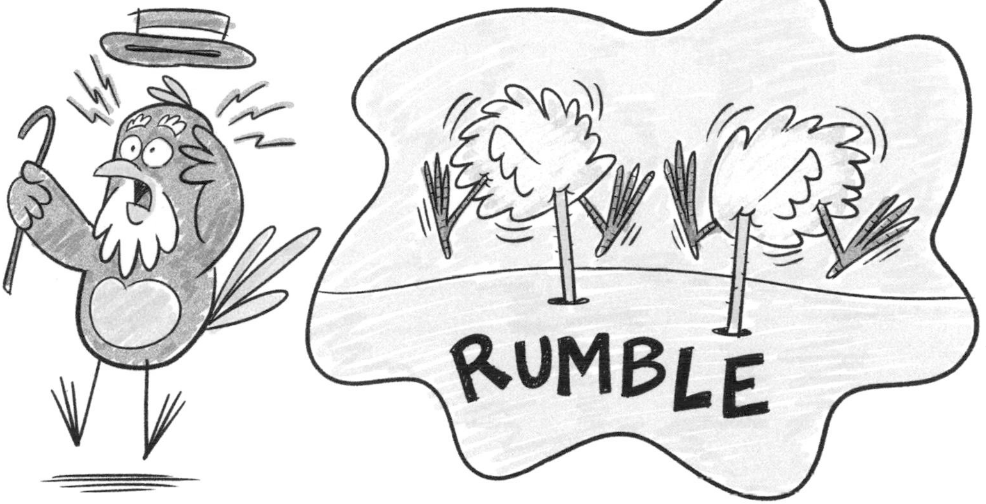
RUMBLE

And the winning lottery numbers back in 1986.

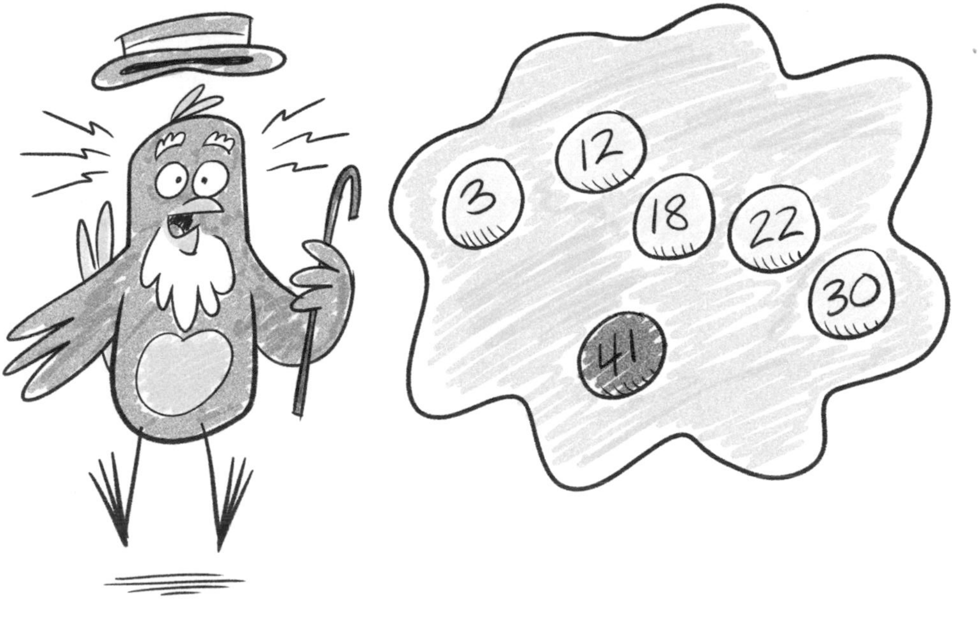
3
12
18
22
30
41

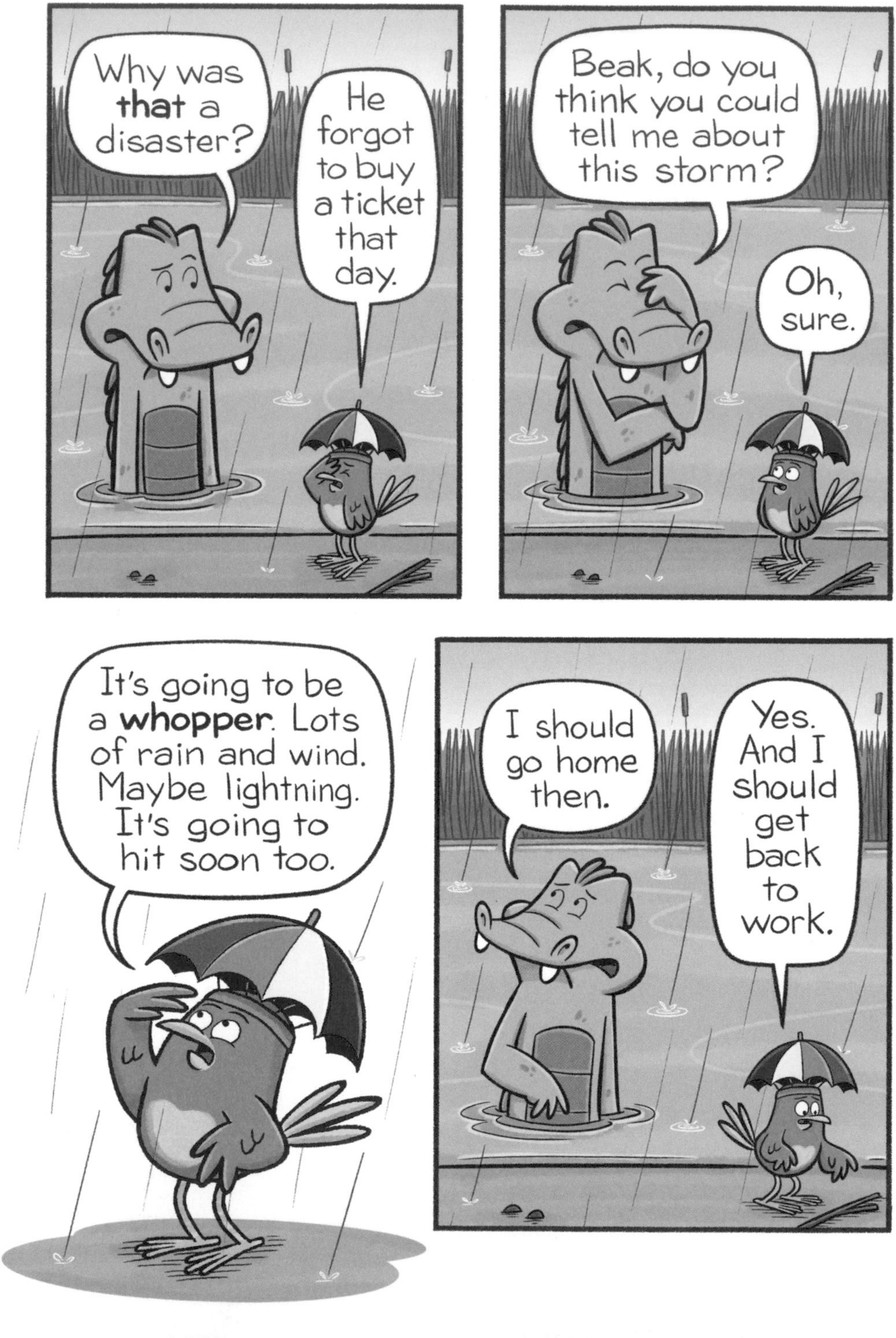
Why was **that** a disaster?
He forgot to buy a ticket that day.
Beak, do you think you could tell me about this storm?
Oh, sure.
It's going to be a **whopper**. Lots of rain and wind. Maybe lightning. It's going to hit soon too.
I should go home then.
Yes. And I should get back to work.

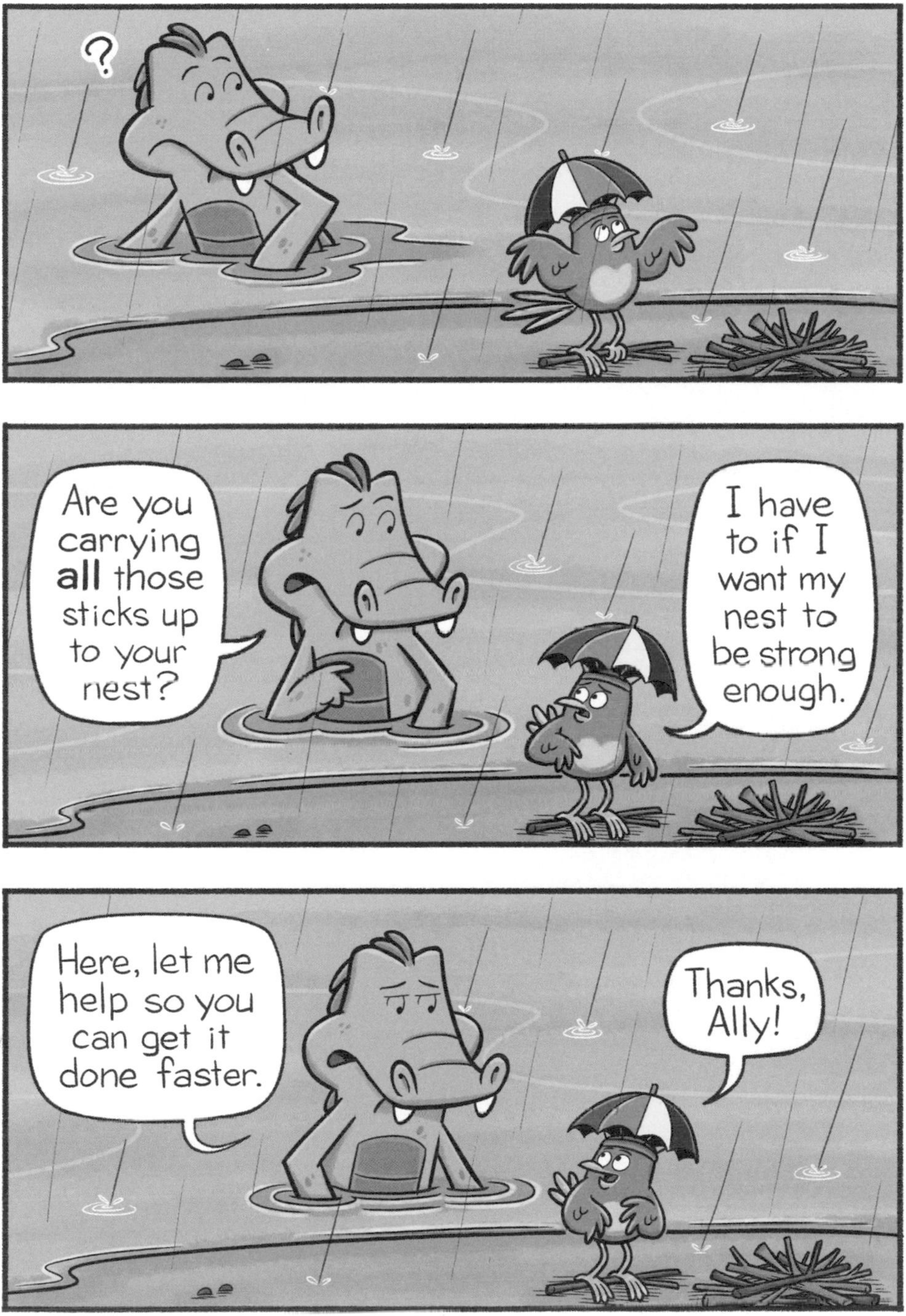
?
Are you carrying **all** those sticks up to your nest?
I have to if I want my nest to be strong enough.
Here, let me help so you can get it done faster.
Thanks, Ally!

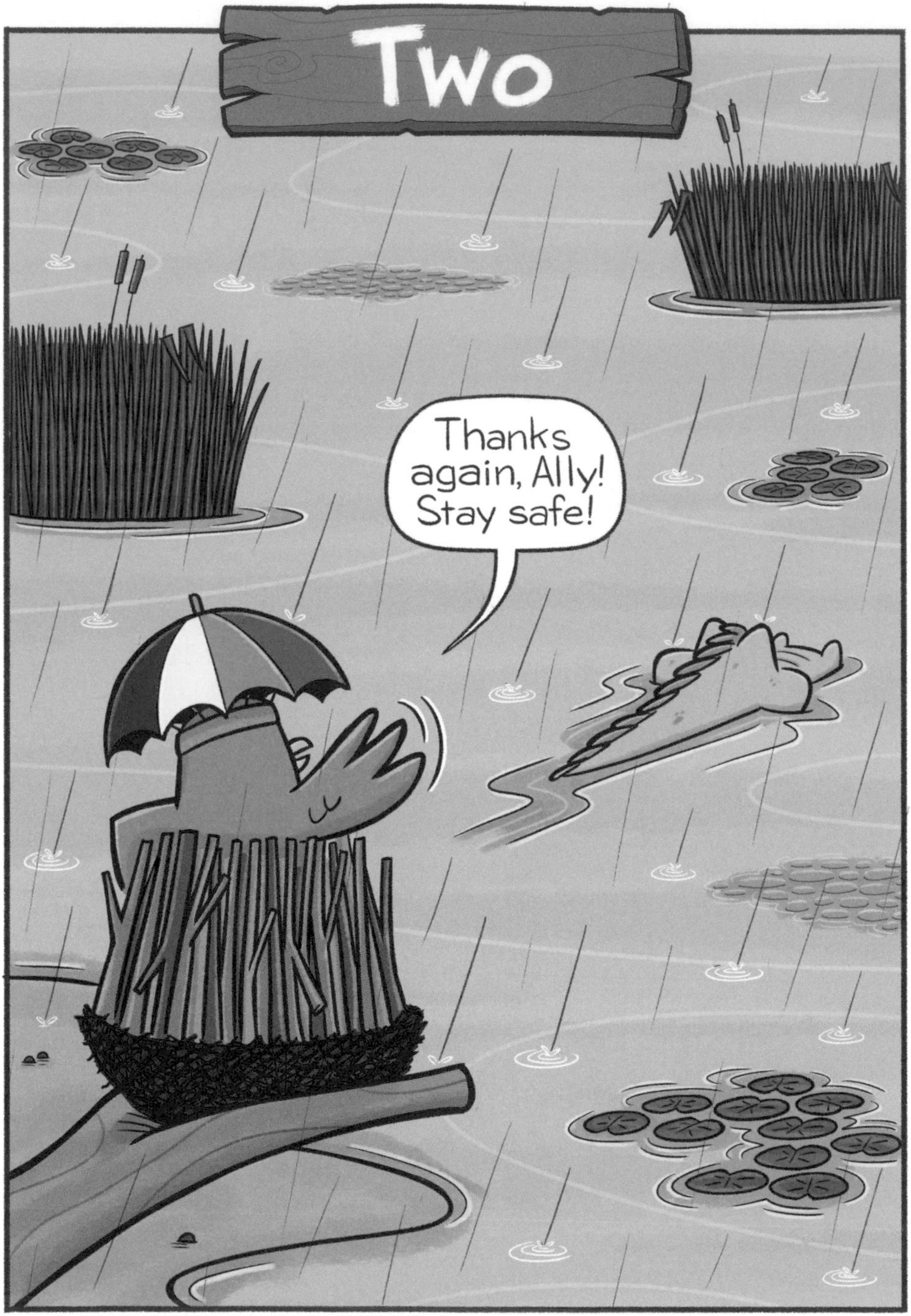
Two
Thanks again, Ally! Stay safe!

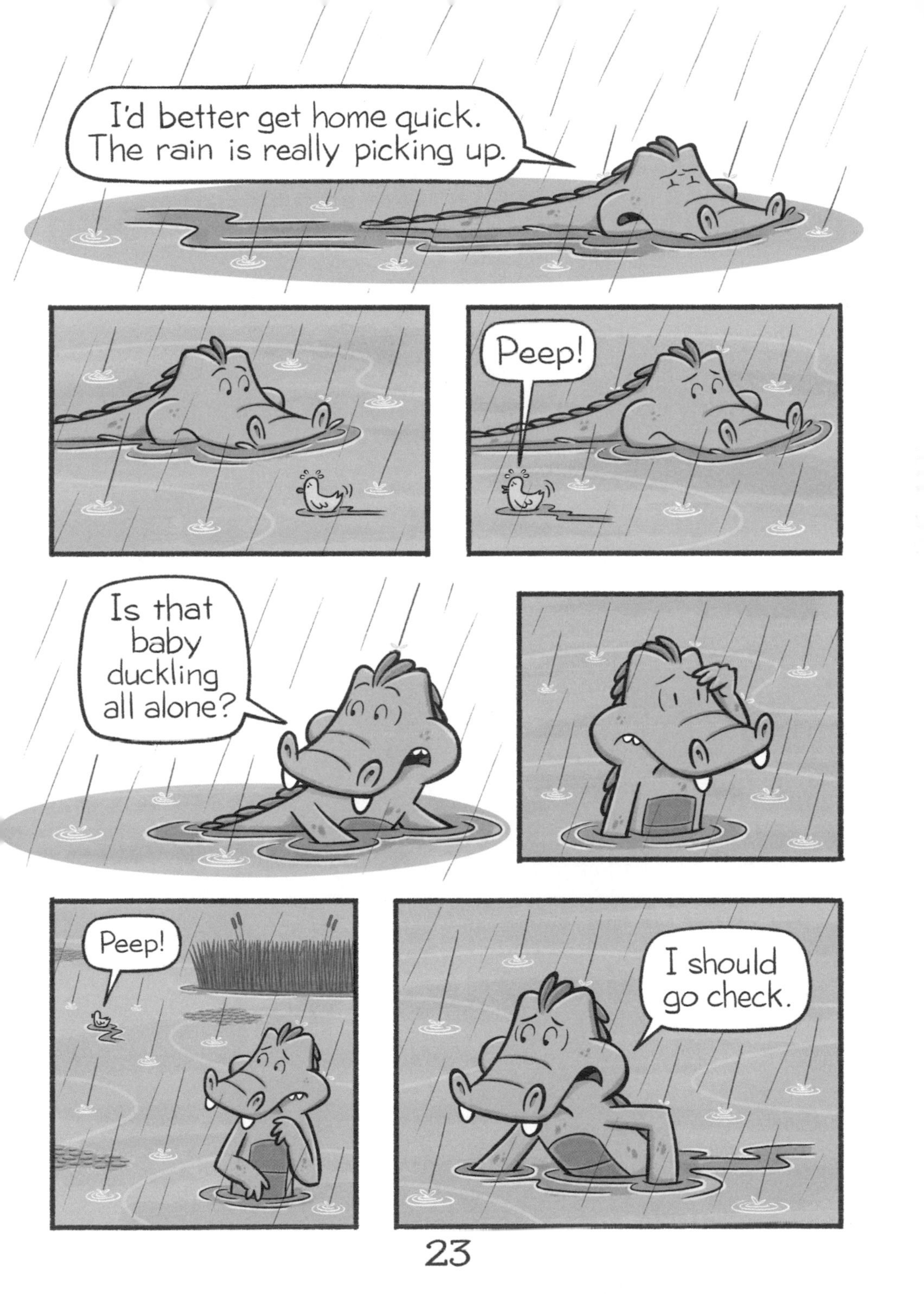
I'd better get home quick. The rain is really picking up.
Peep!
Is that baby duckling all alone?
Peep!
I should go check.

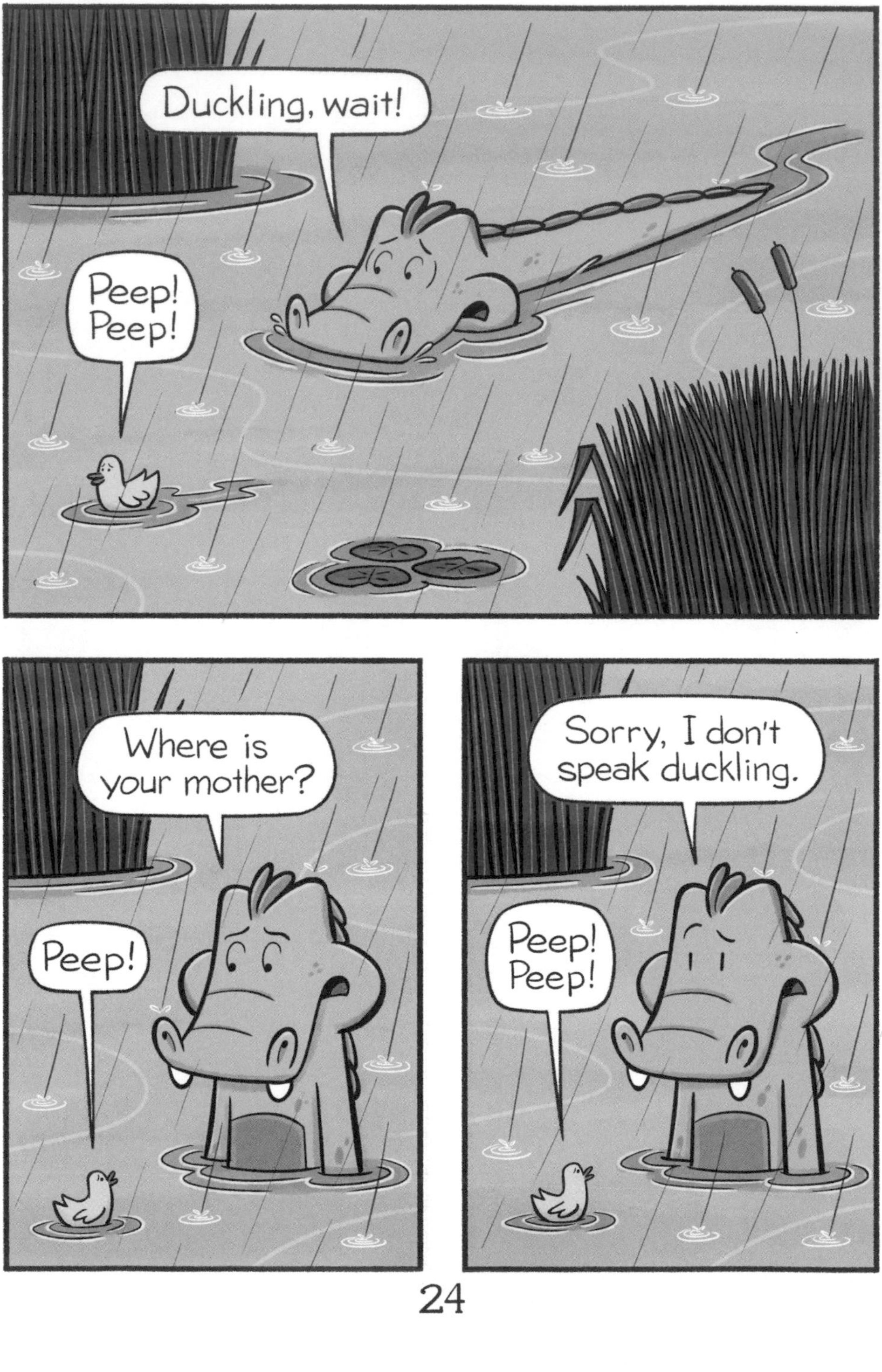
Duckling, wait!
Peep! Peep!
Where is your mother?
Peep!
Sorry, I don't speak duckling.
Peep! Peep!

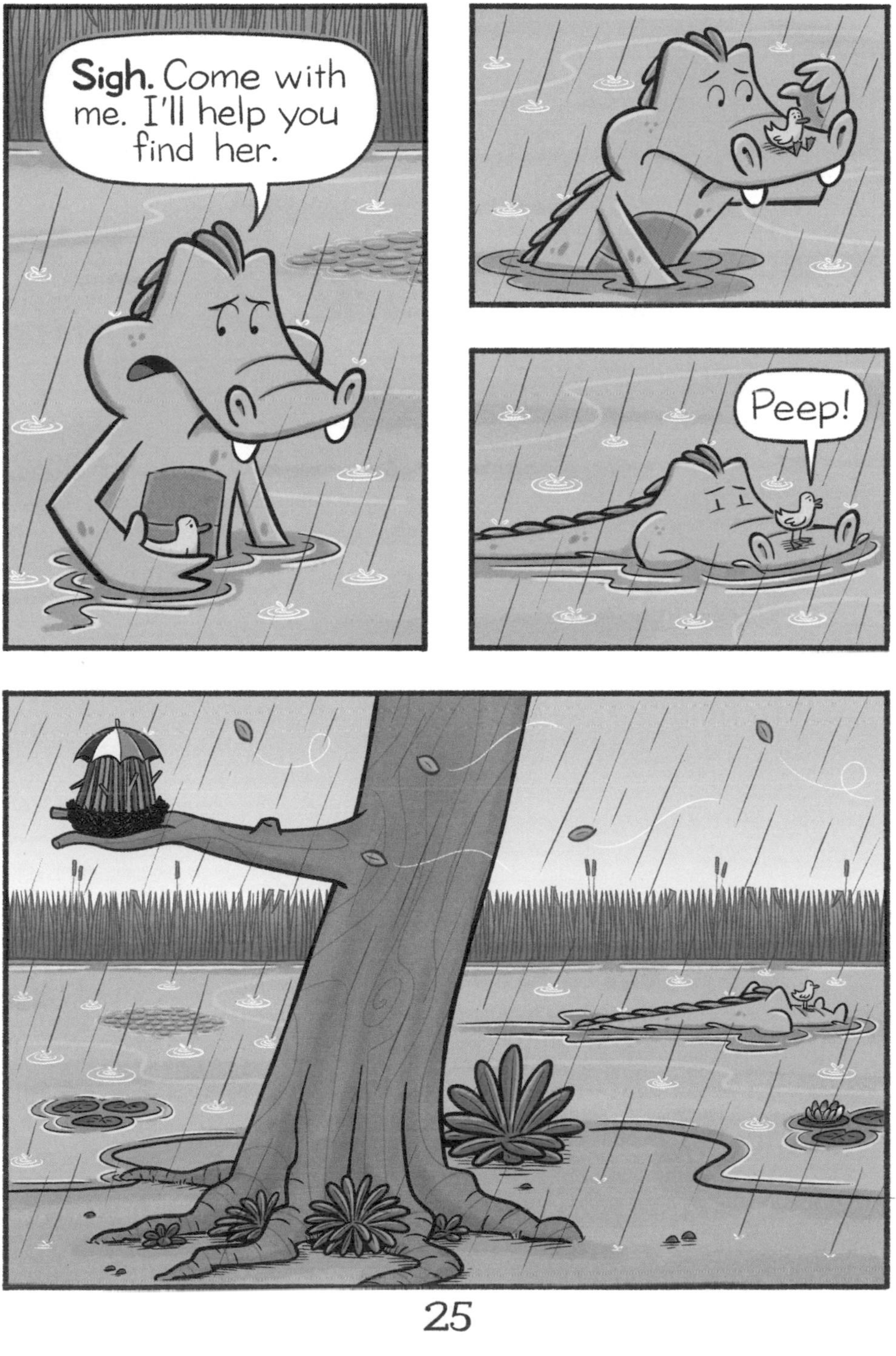
Sigh. Come with me. I'll help you find her.
Peep!

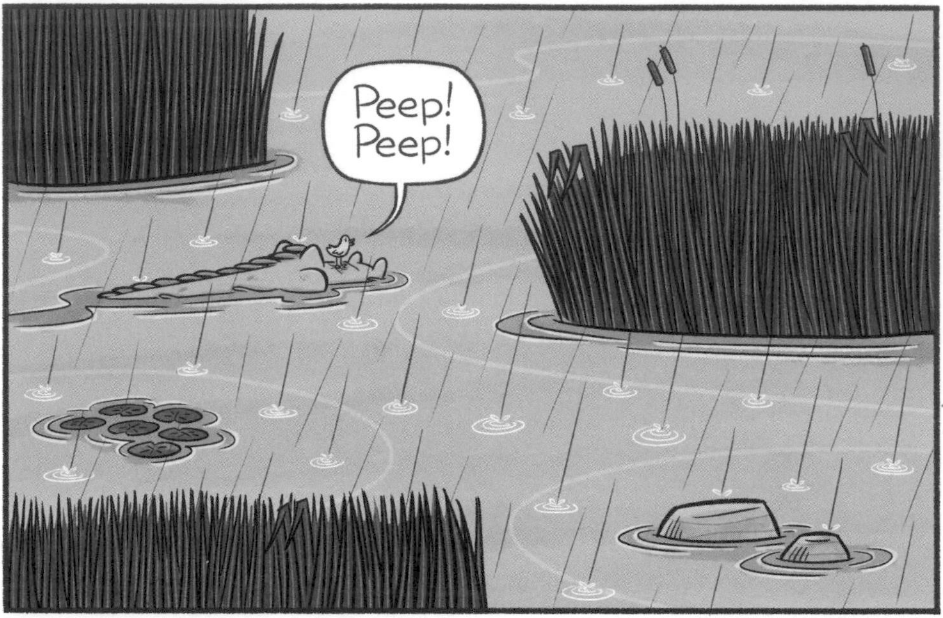
Peep!
Peep!

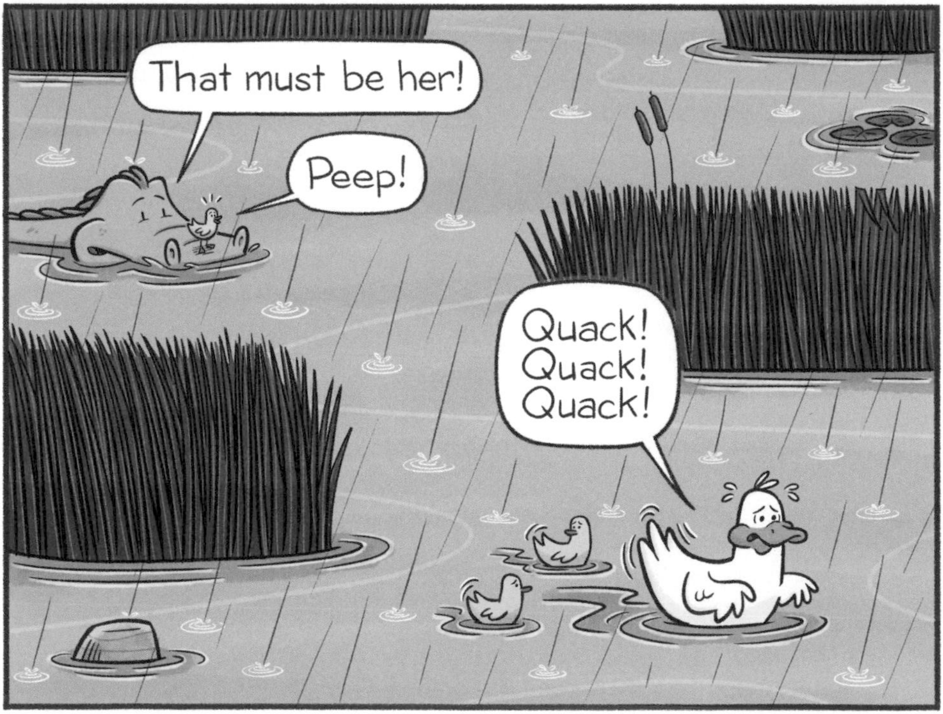
That must be her!
Peep!
Quack!
Quack!
Quack!

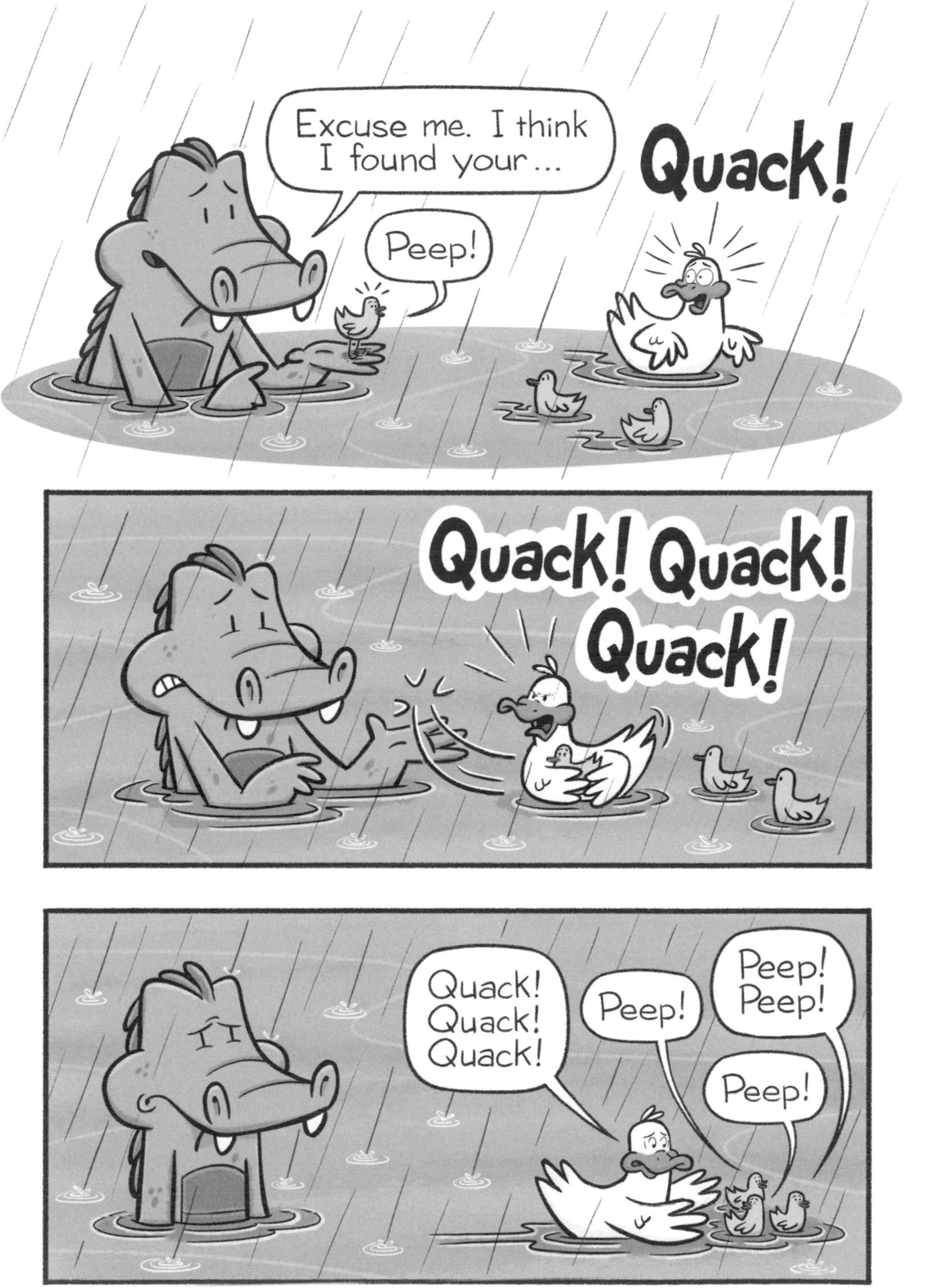

Excuse me. I think I found your...
Peep!
Quack!
Quack! Quack! Quack!
Quack! Quack! Quack!
Peep!
Peep! Peep!
Peep!

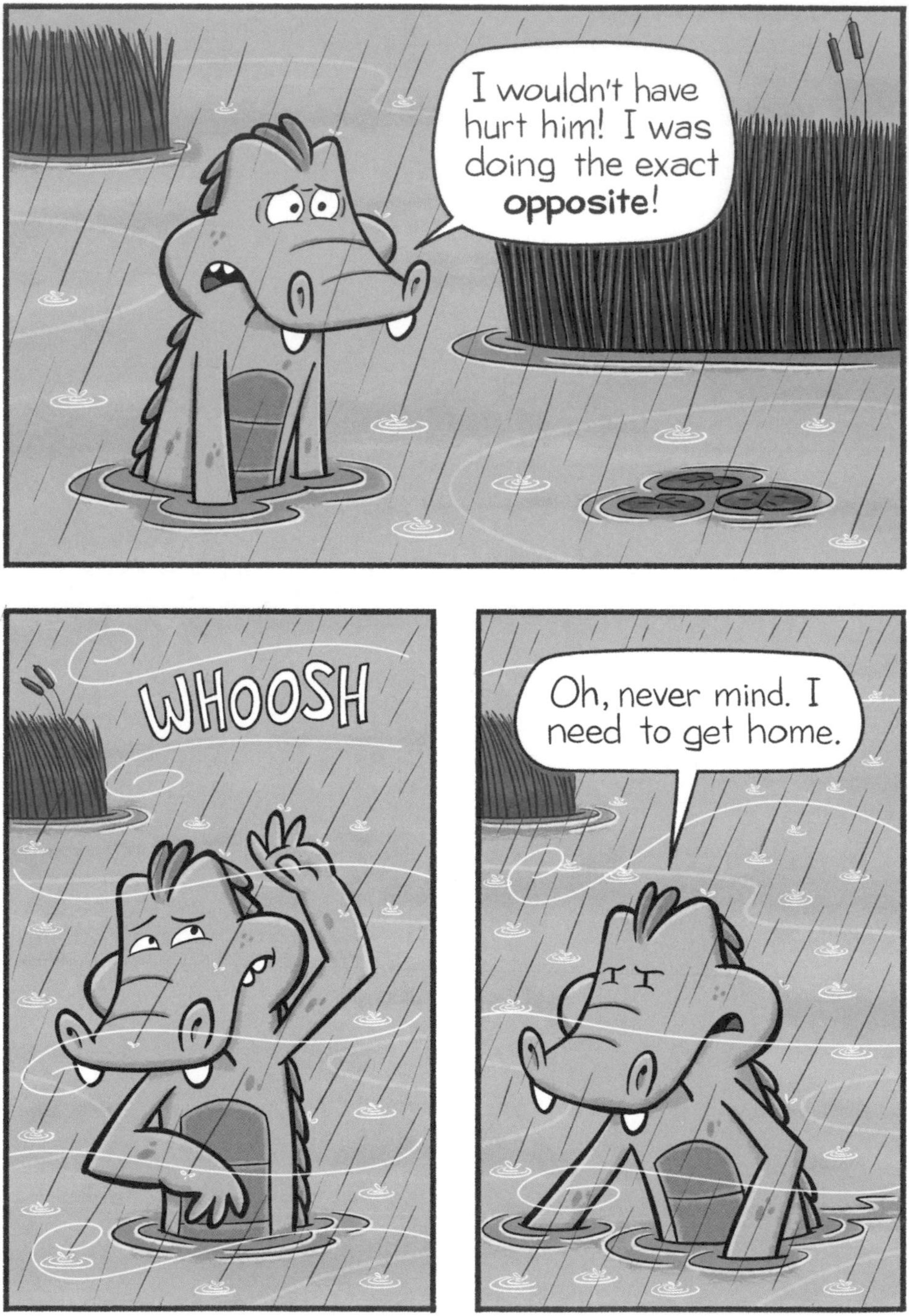
I wouldn't have hurt him! I was doing the exact **opposite**!
WHOOSH
Oh, never mind. I need to get home.

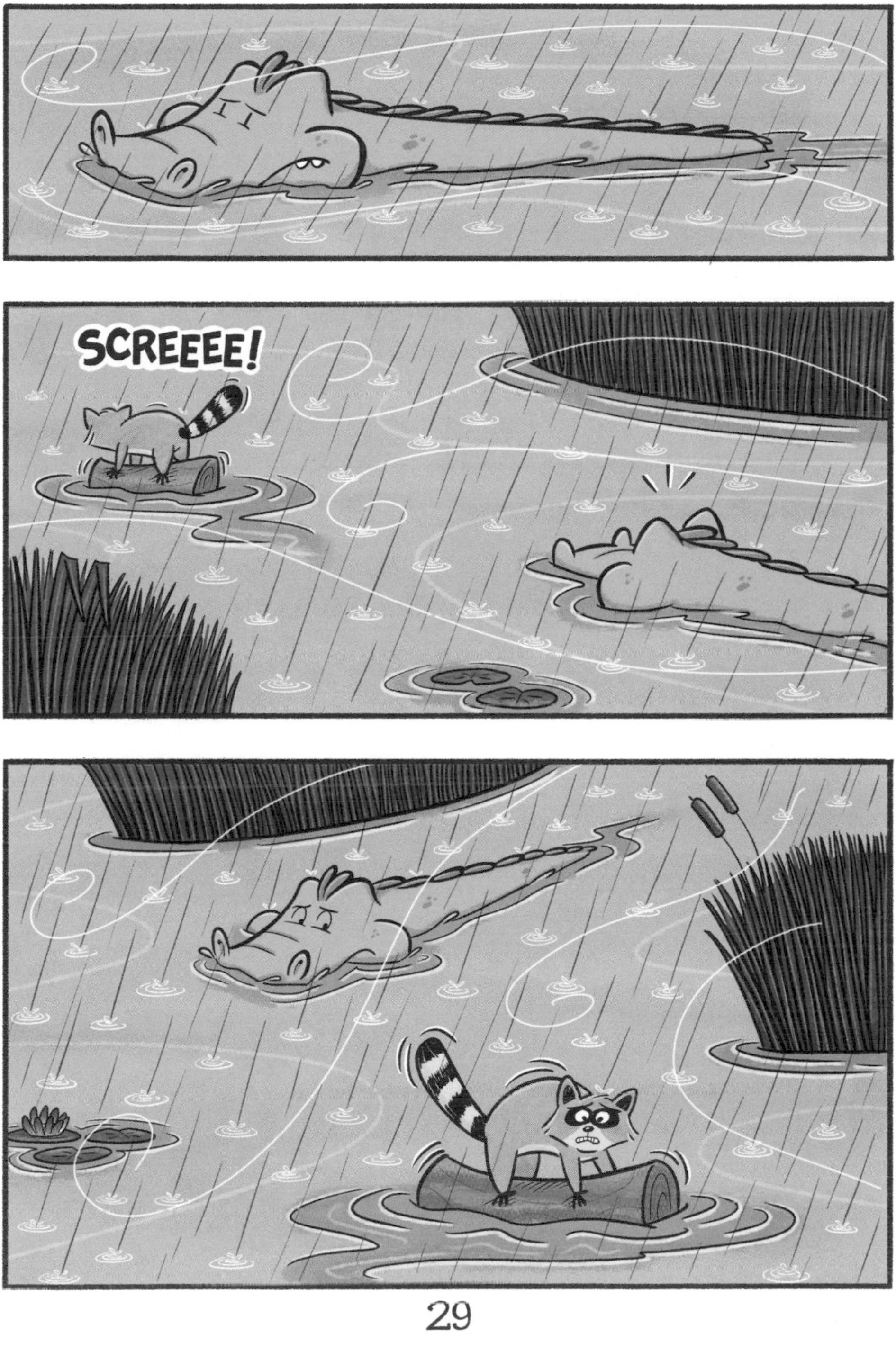
SCREEEE!

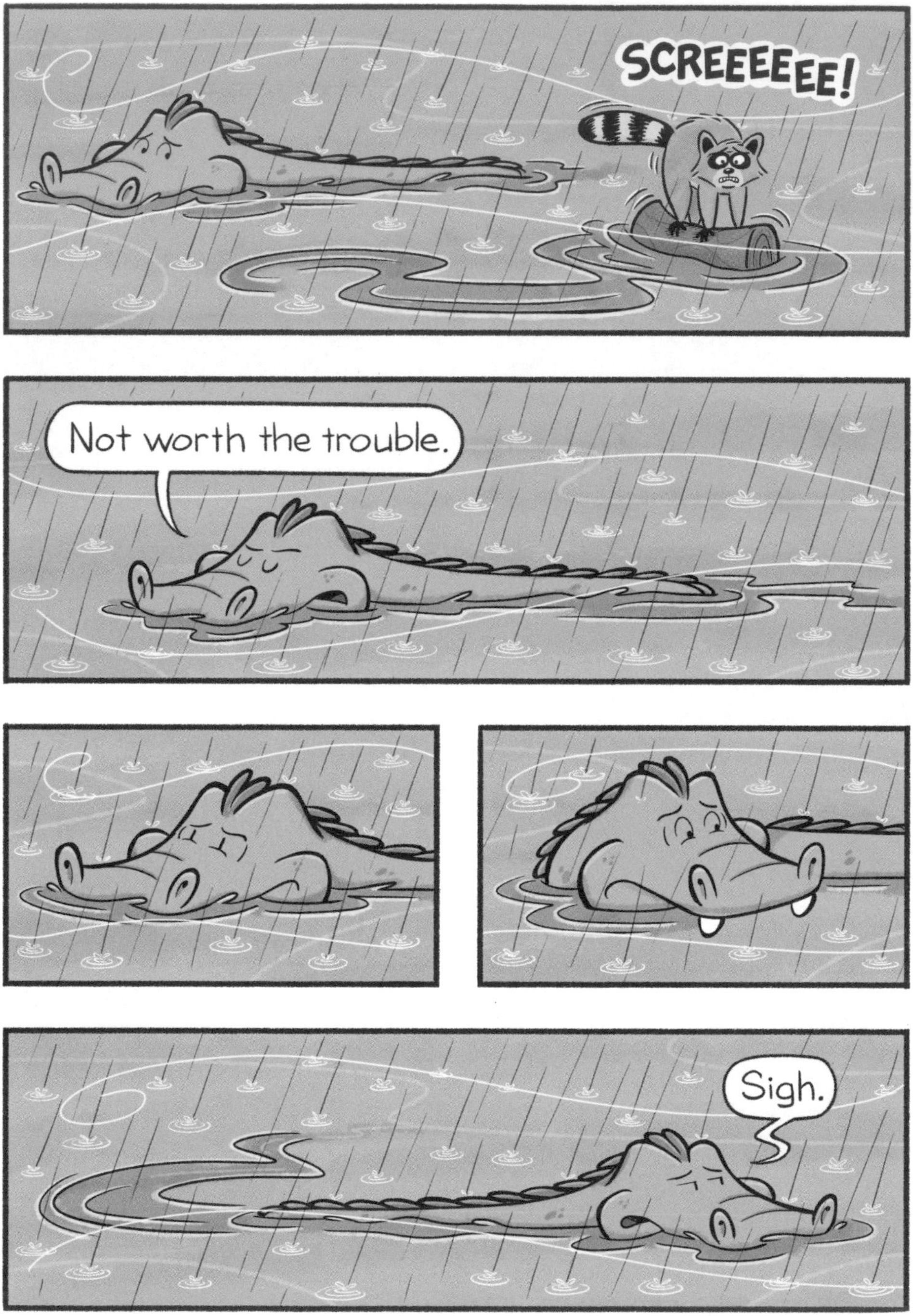
SCREEEEEEE!
Not worth the trouble.
Sigh.

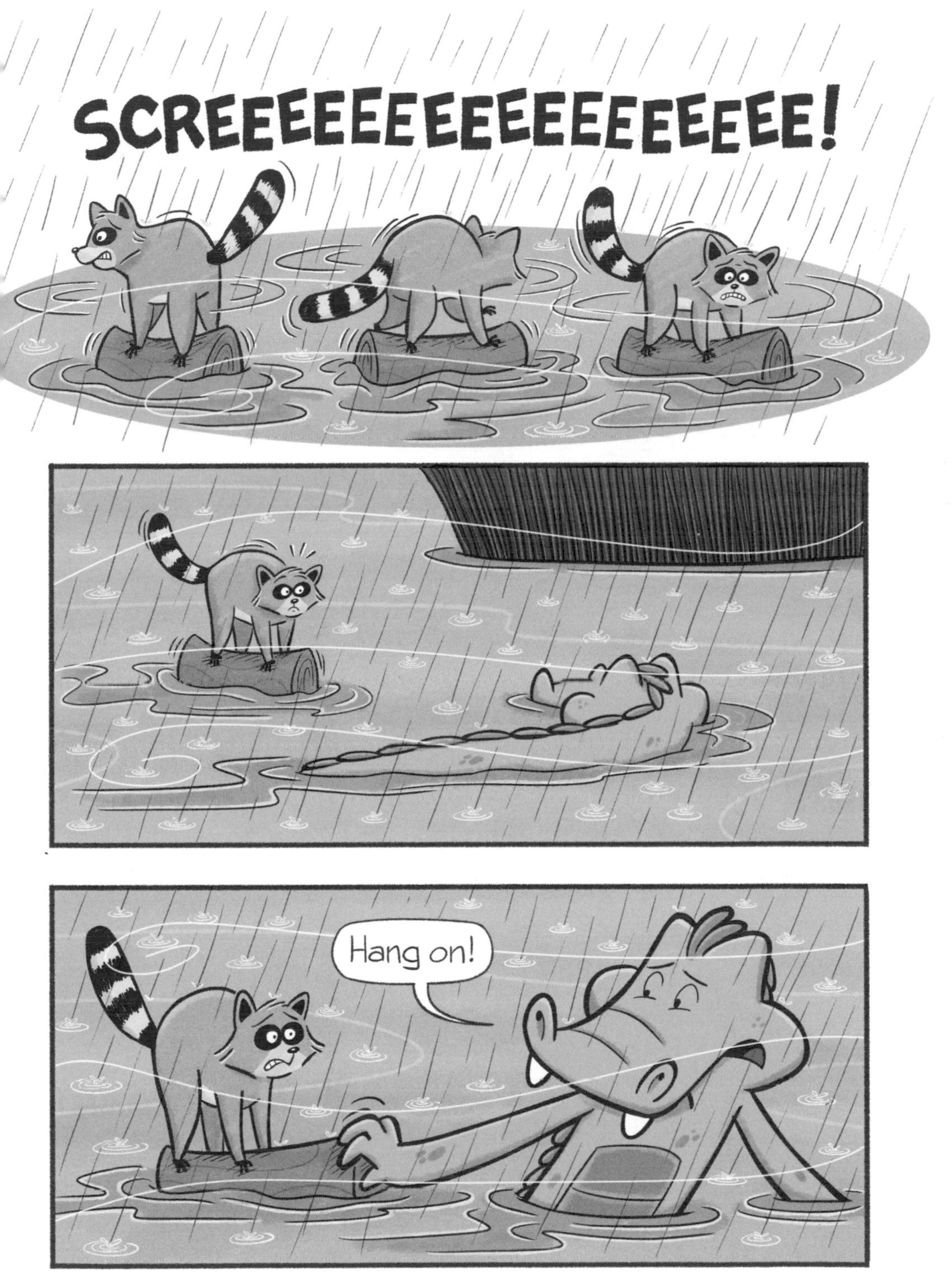
SCREEEEEEEEEEEEEEEEEE!
Hang on!

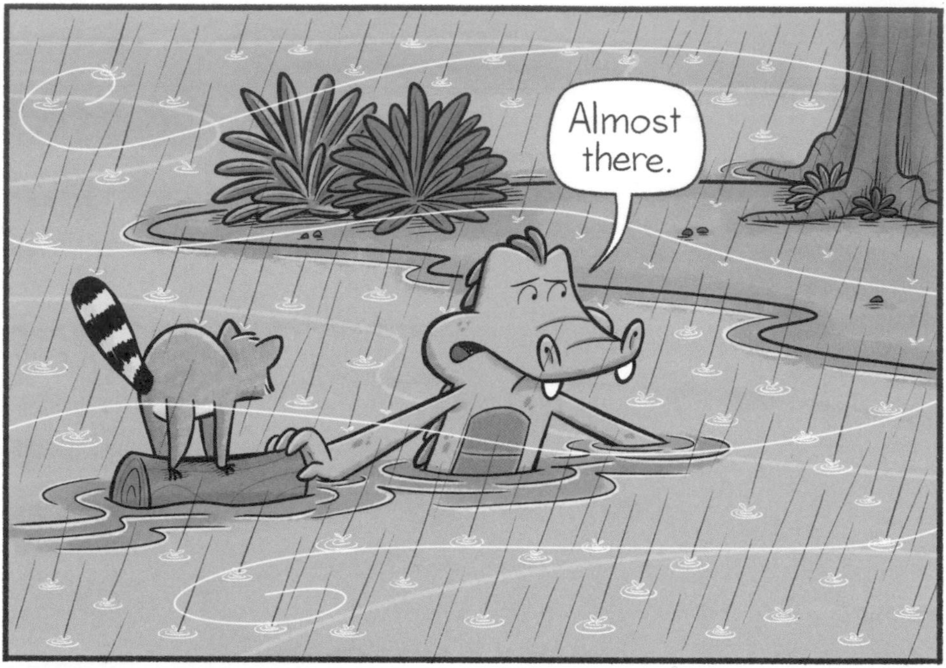
Almost there.

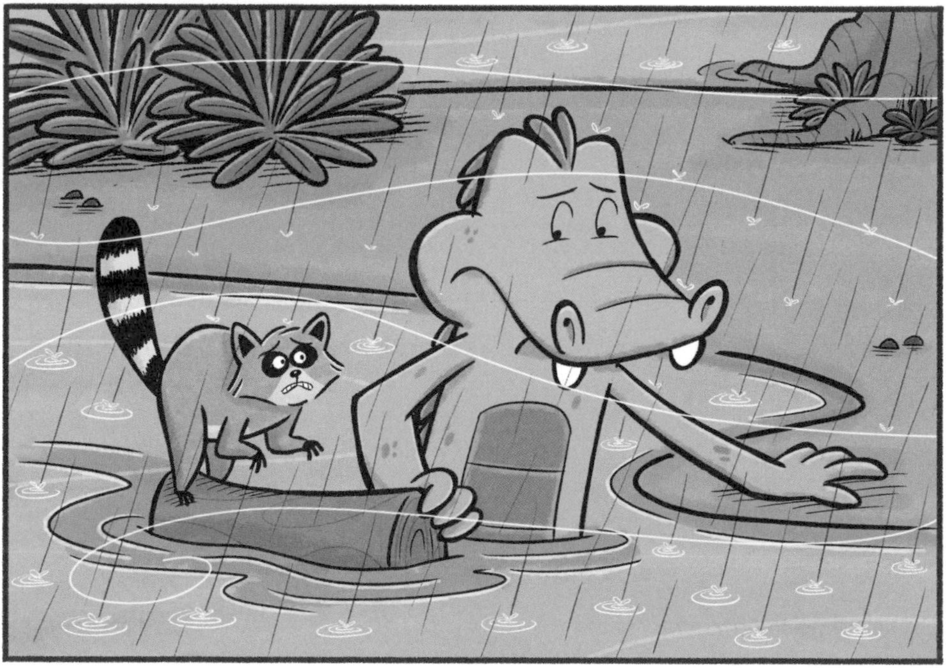

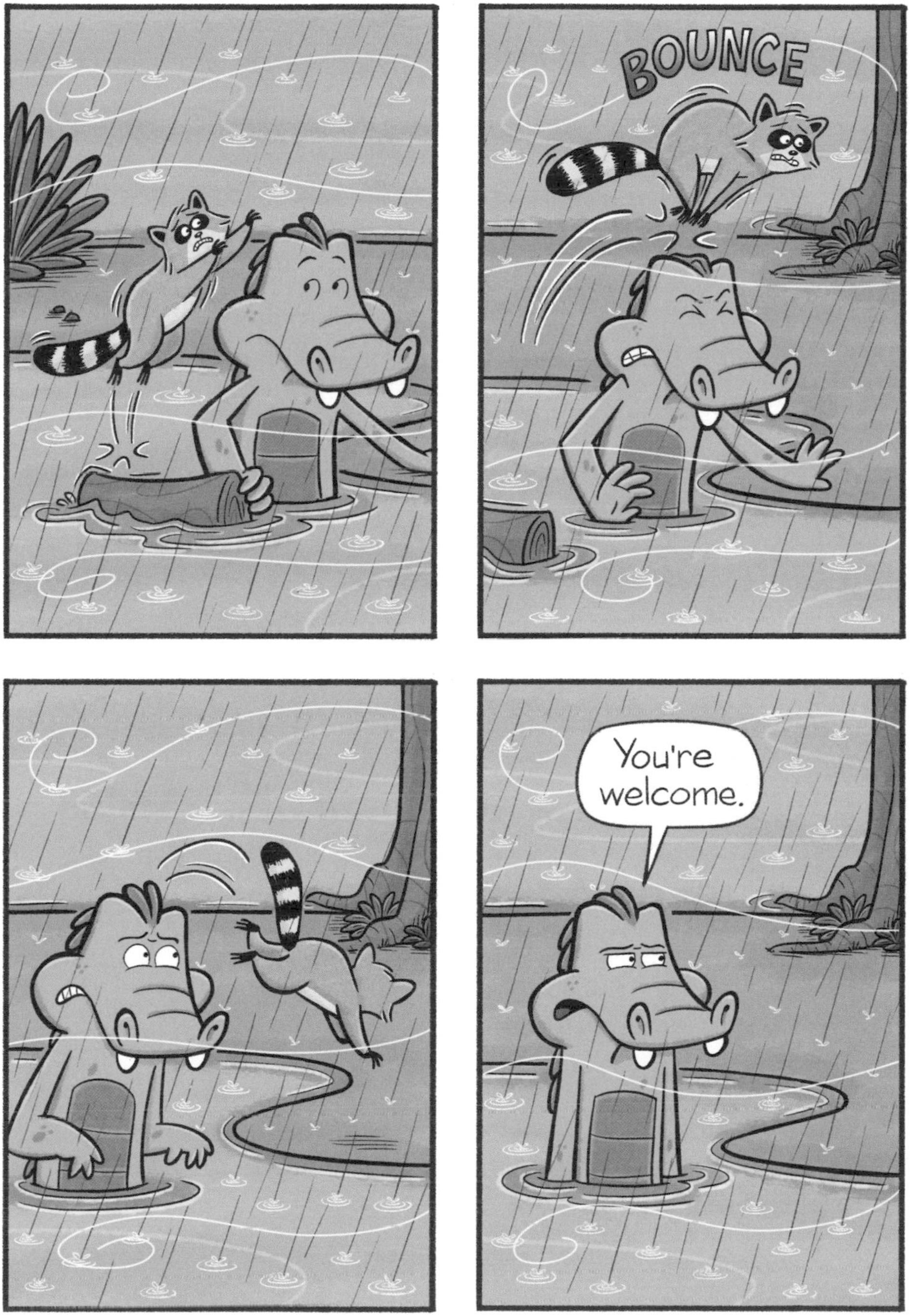
BOUNCE
You're welcome.

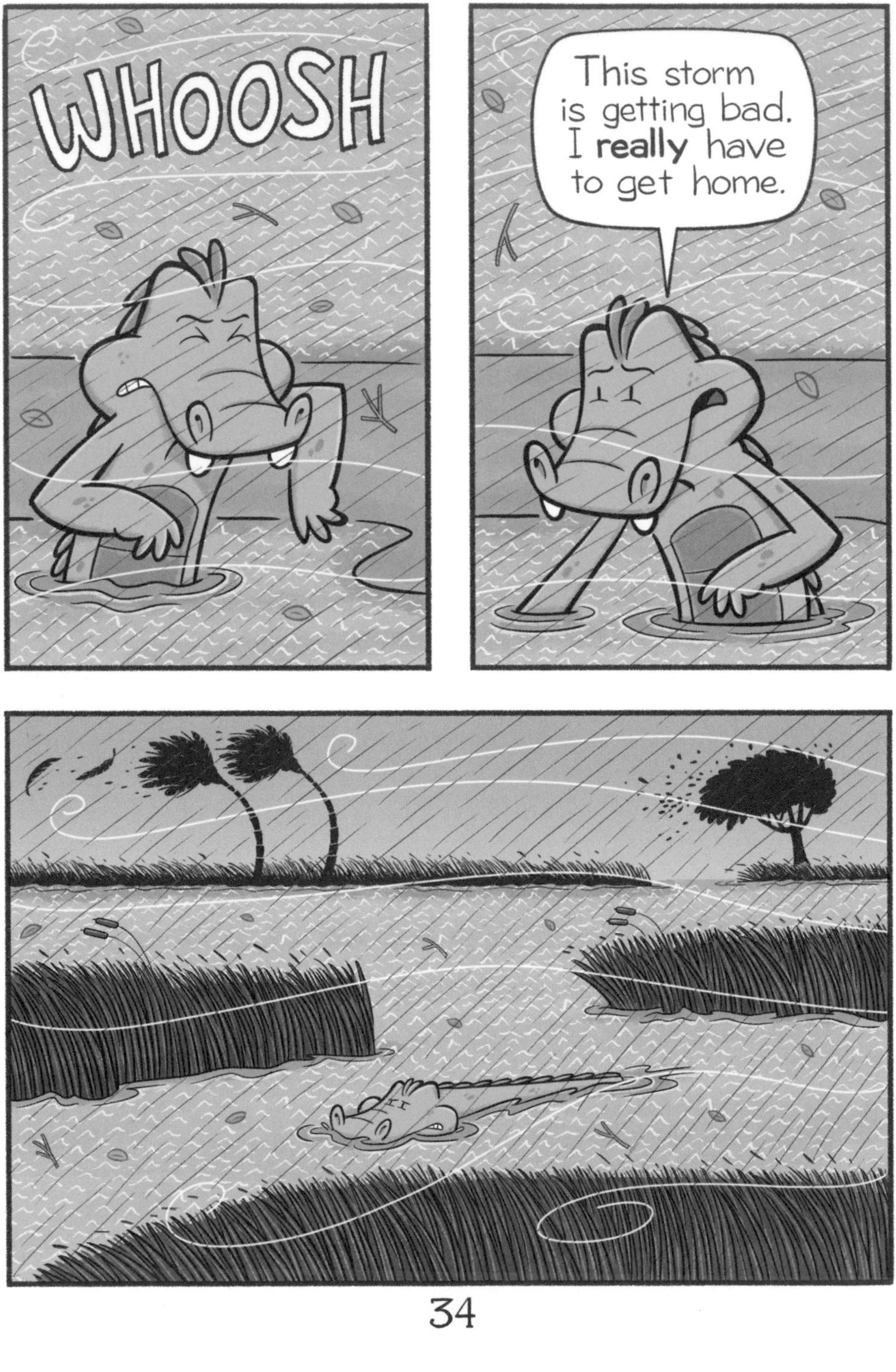
WHOOSH
This storm is getting bad. I **really** have to get home.

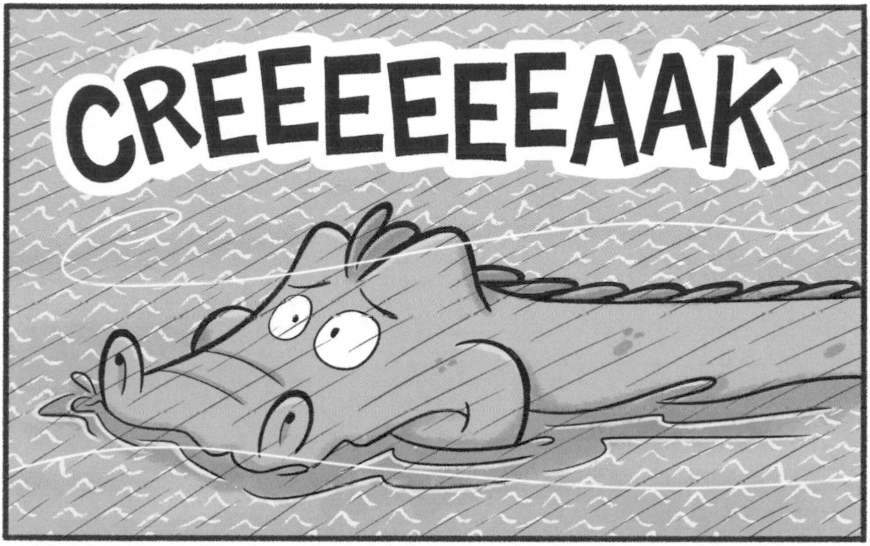
CREEEEEEEAAK

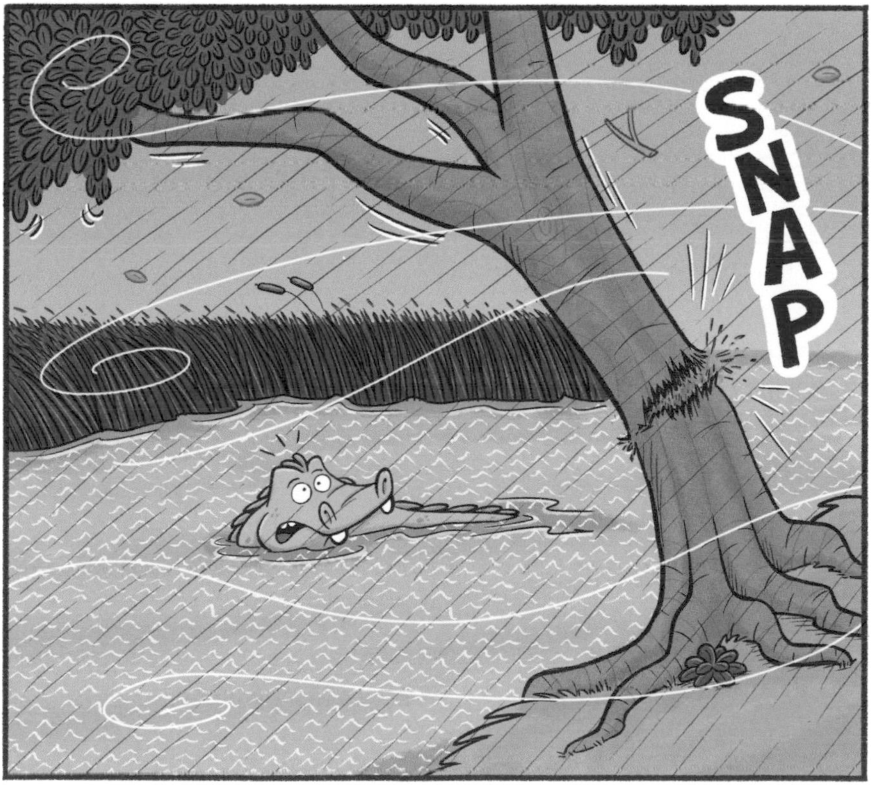
SNAP

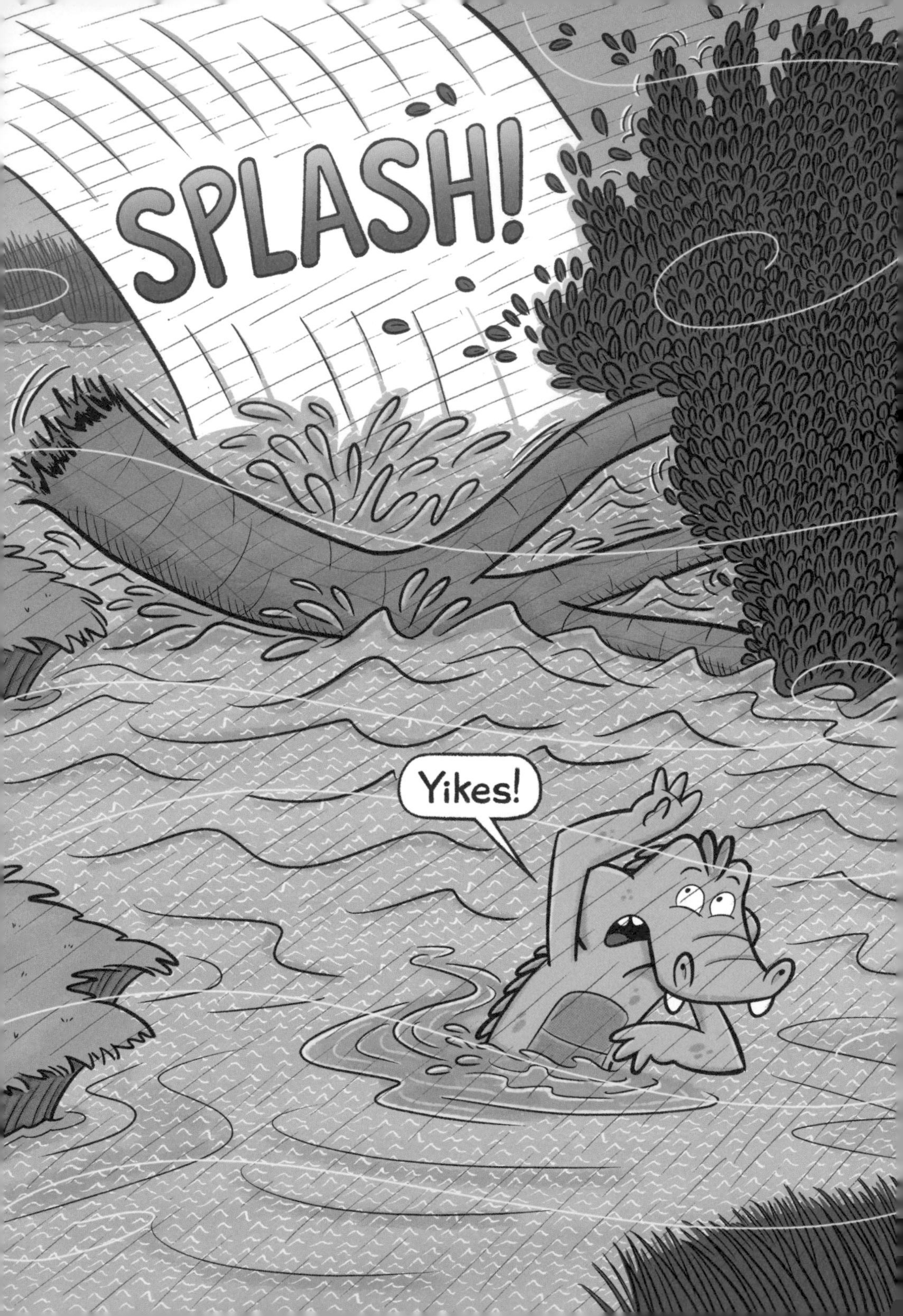
SPLASH!
Yikes!

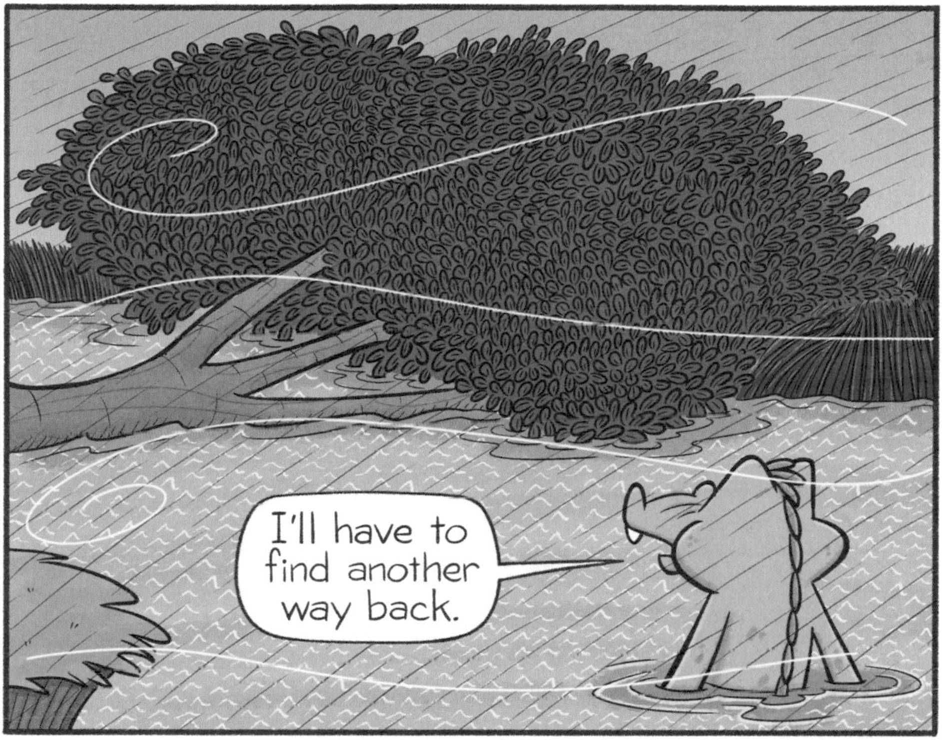
I'll have to find another way back.

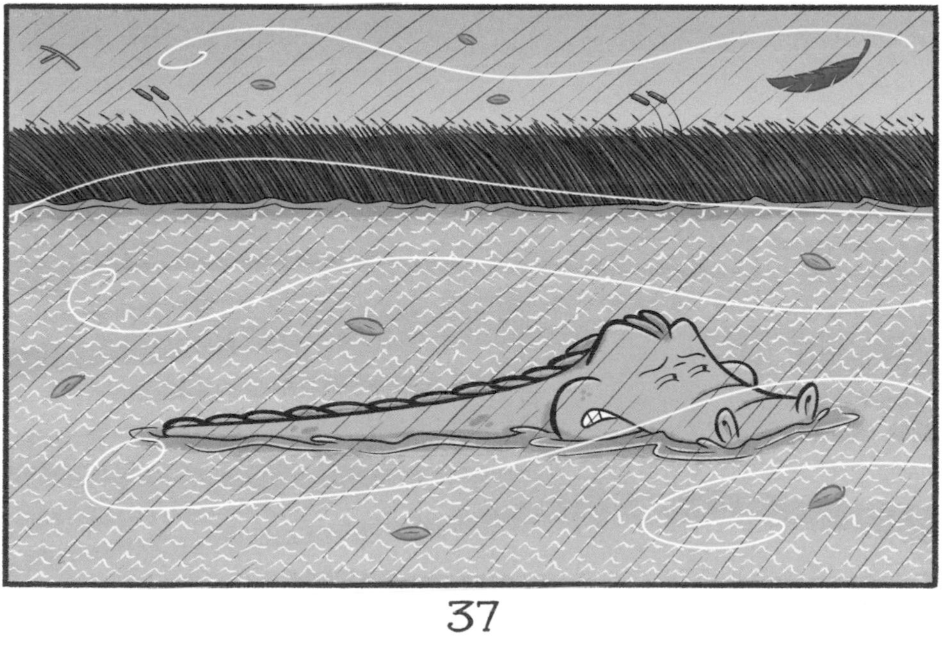

It's no use. I'll never make it home now.
WHOOSH
I'd better find shelter for the night.

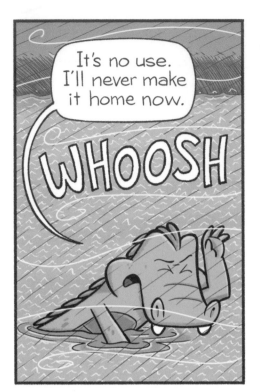

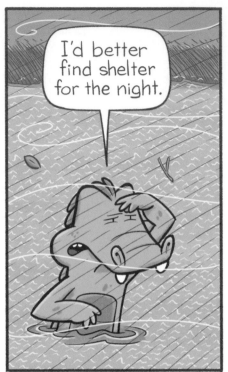

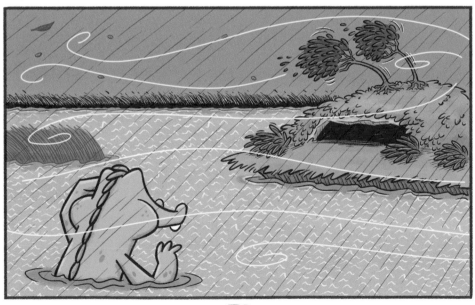

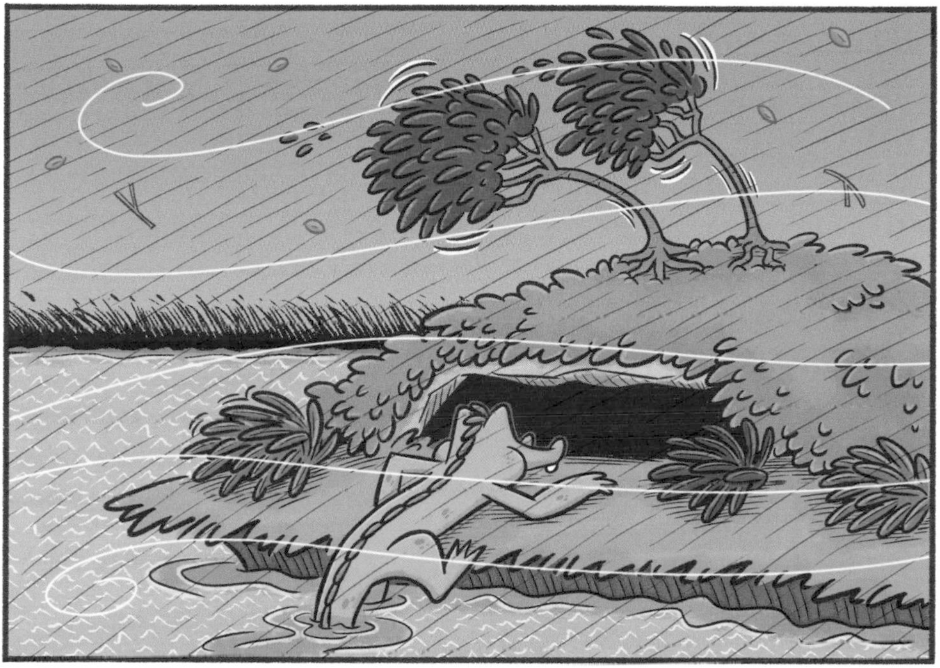

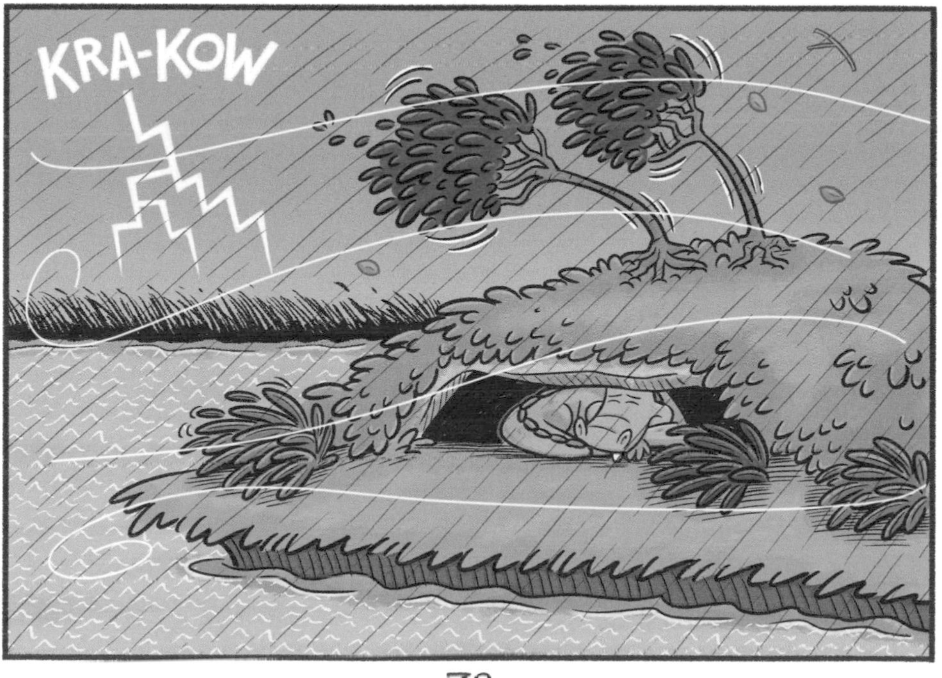
KRA-KOW

Three

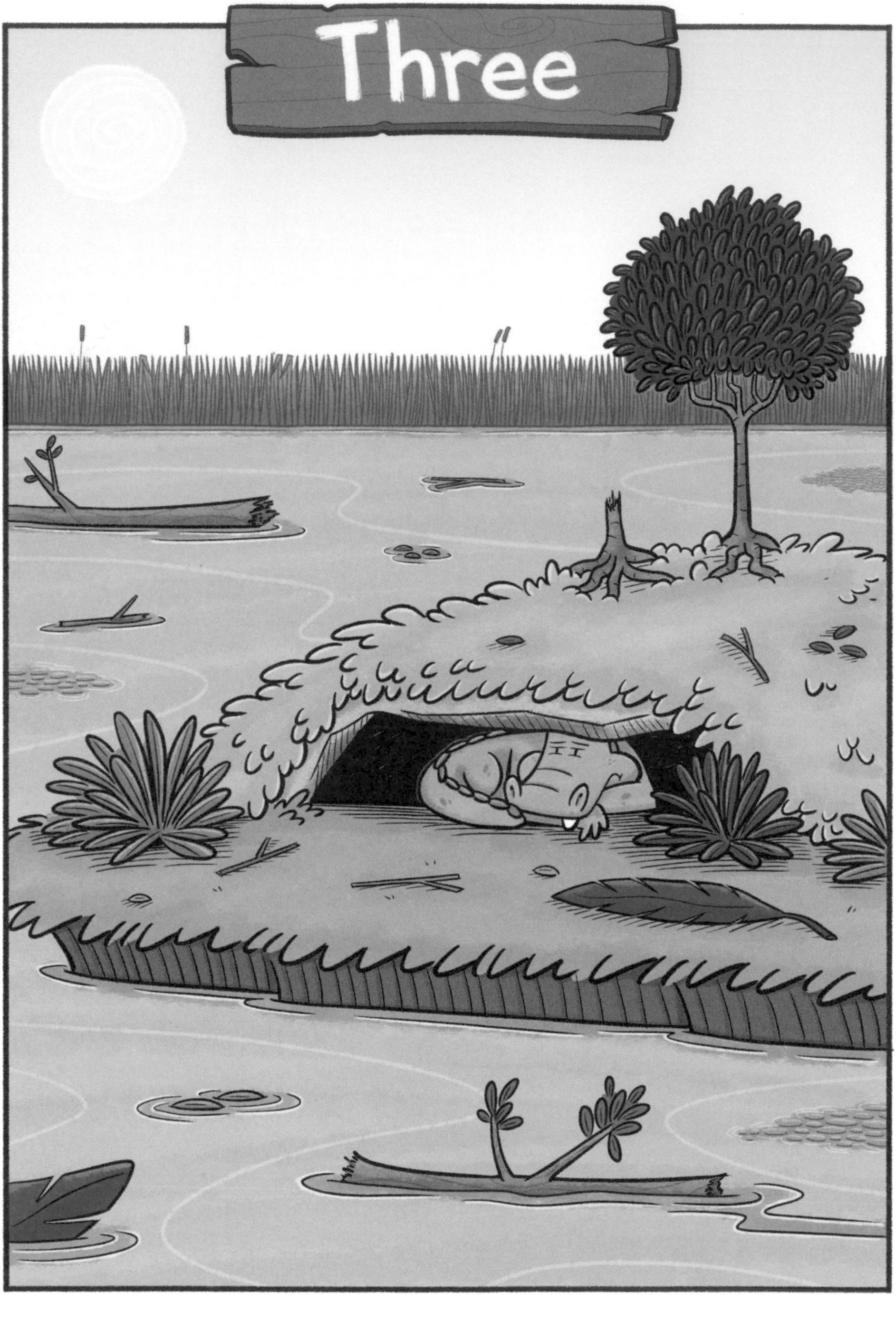

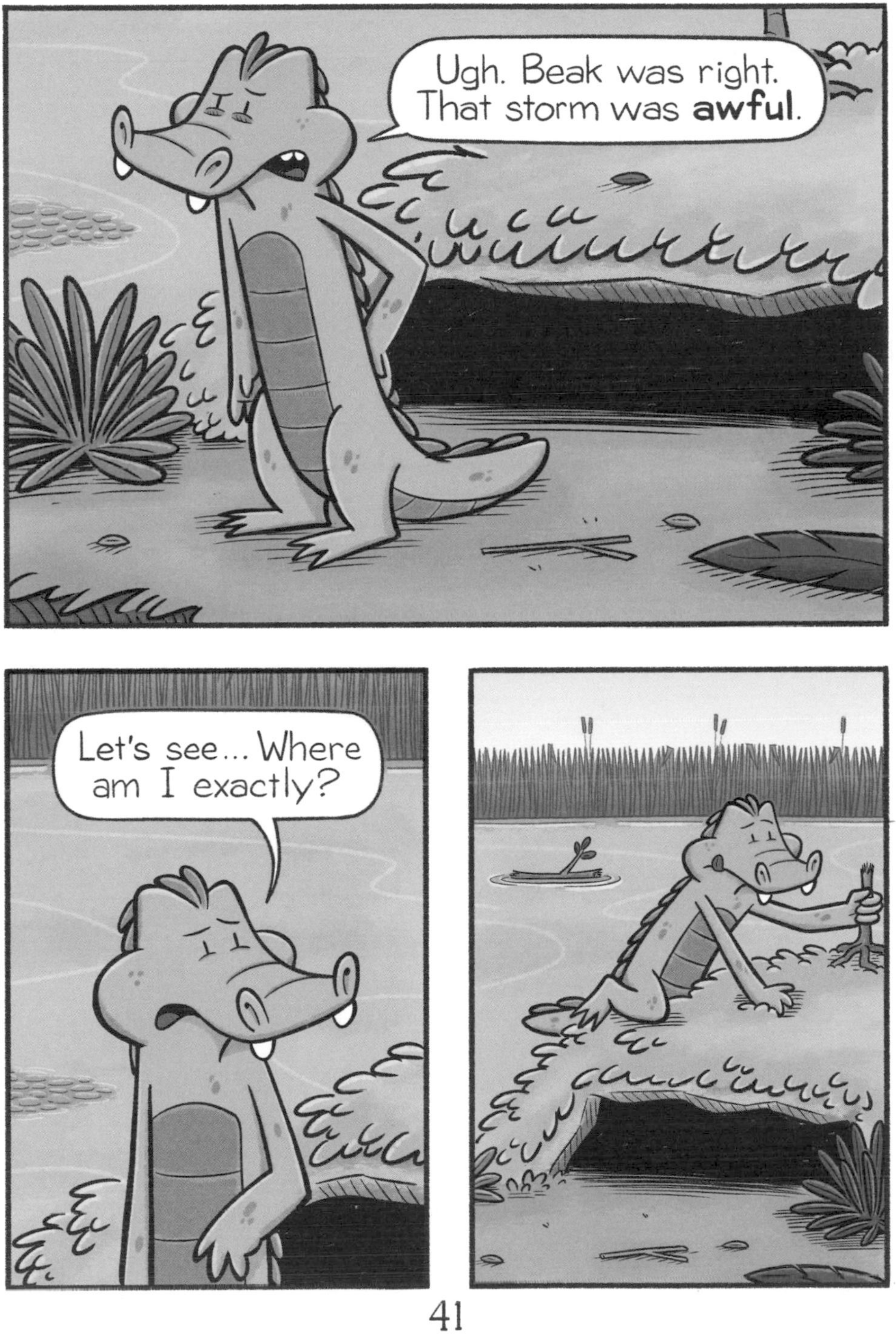
Ugh. Beak was right. That storm was **awful**.
Let's see... Where am I exactly?

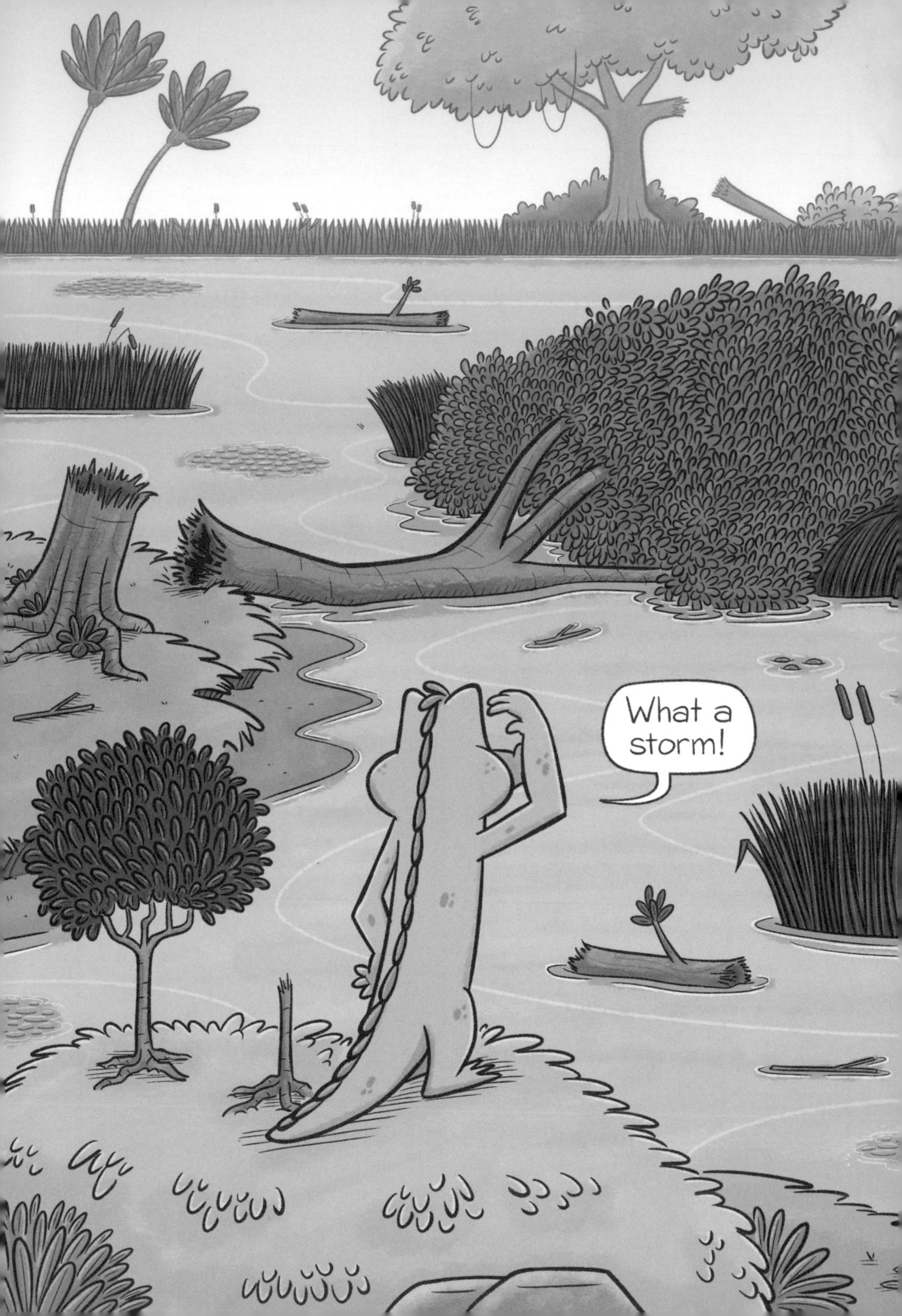
What a storm!

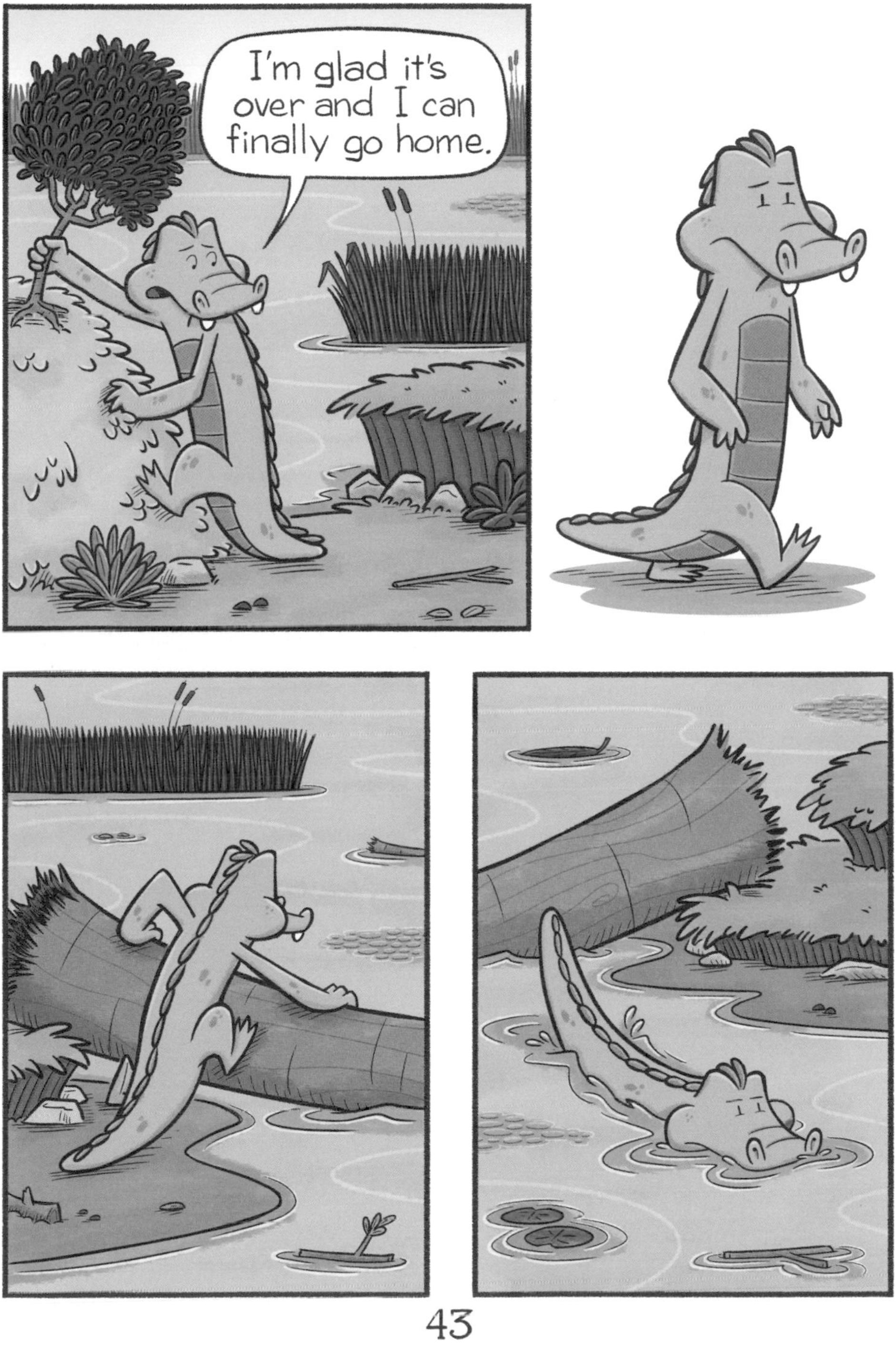
I'm glad it's over and I can finally go home.

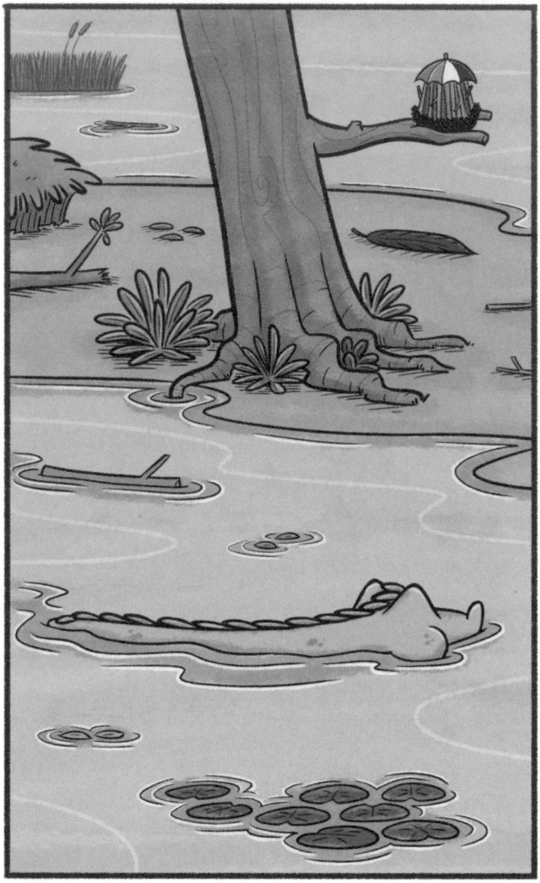

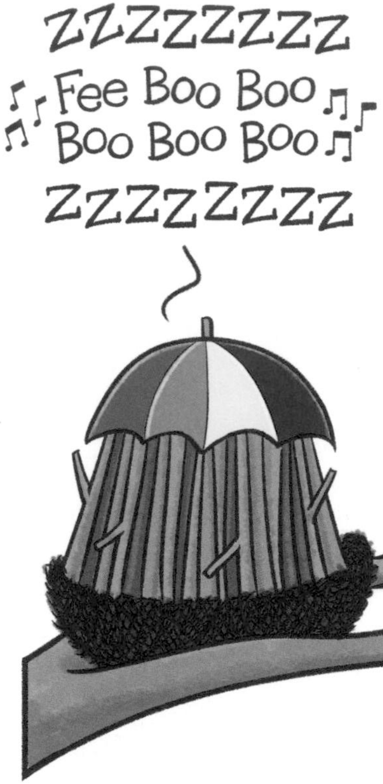
ZZZZZZZZ
Fee Boo Boo
Boo Boo Boo
ZZZZZZZZ

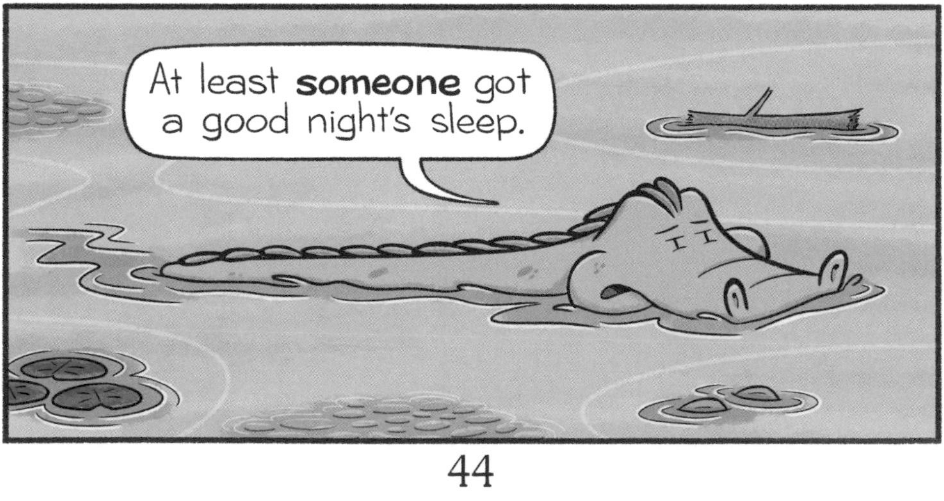
At least **someone** got a good night's sleep.

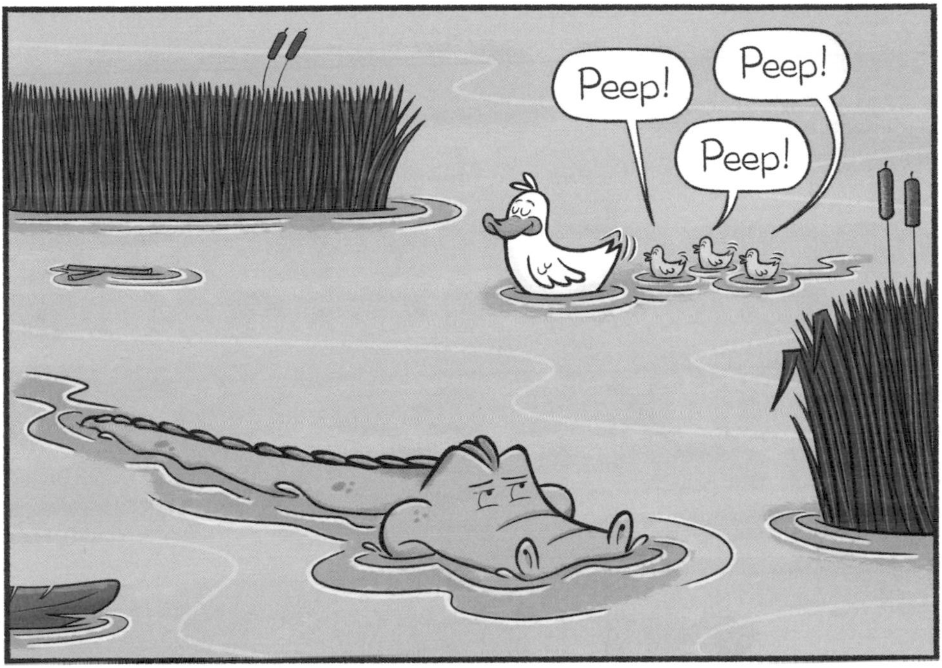
Peep!
Peep!
Peep!

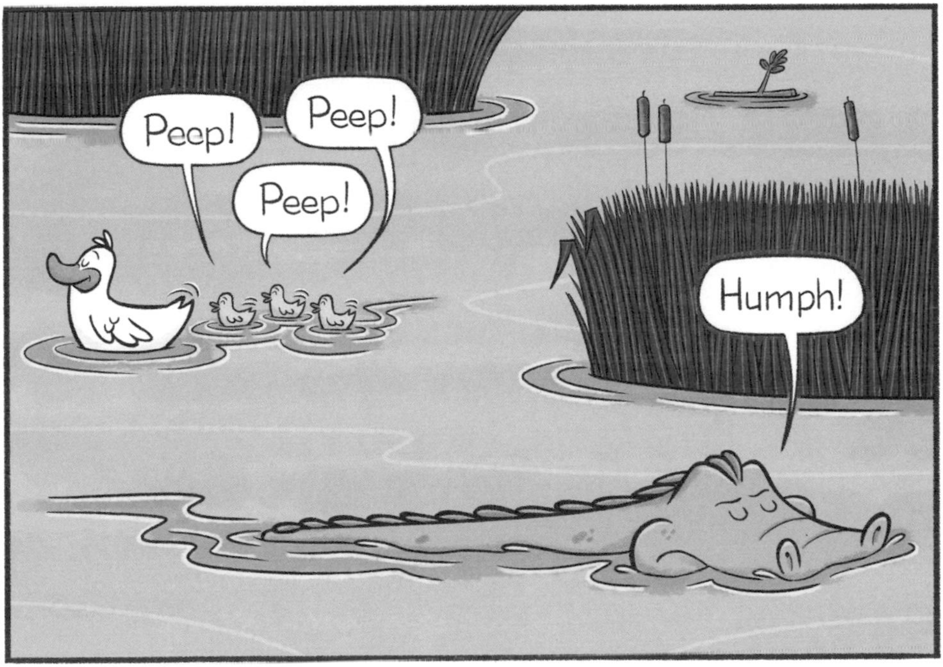
Peep!
Peep!
Peep!
Humph!

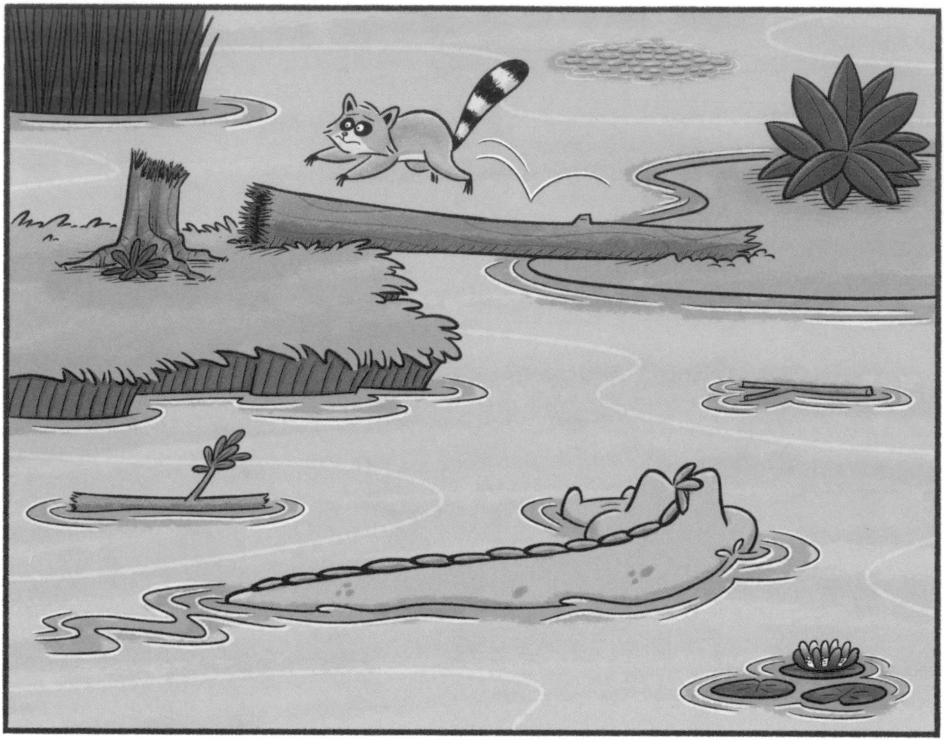

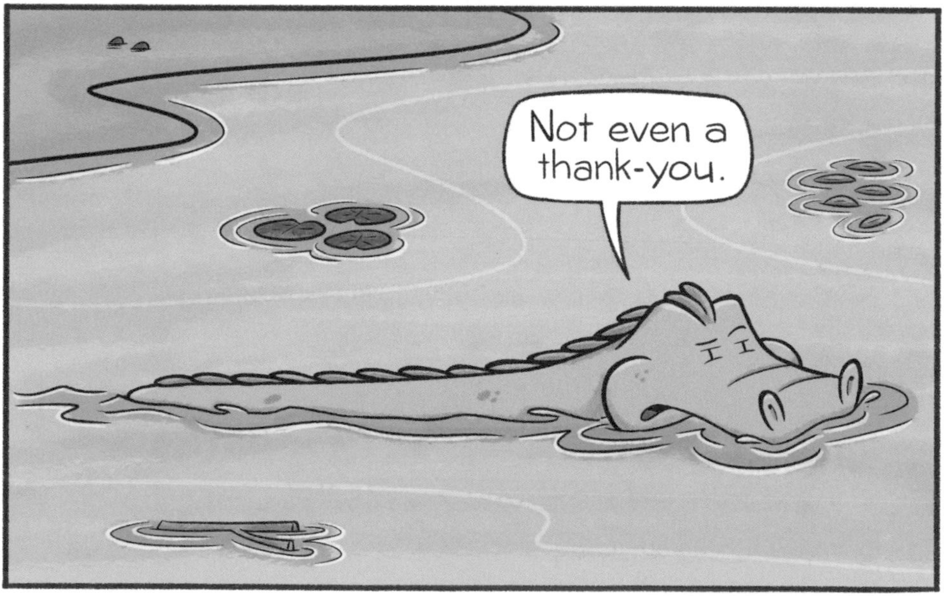
Not even a thank-you.

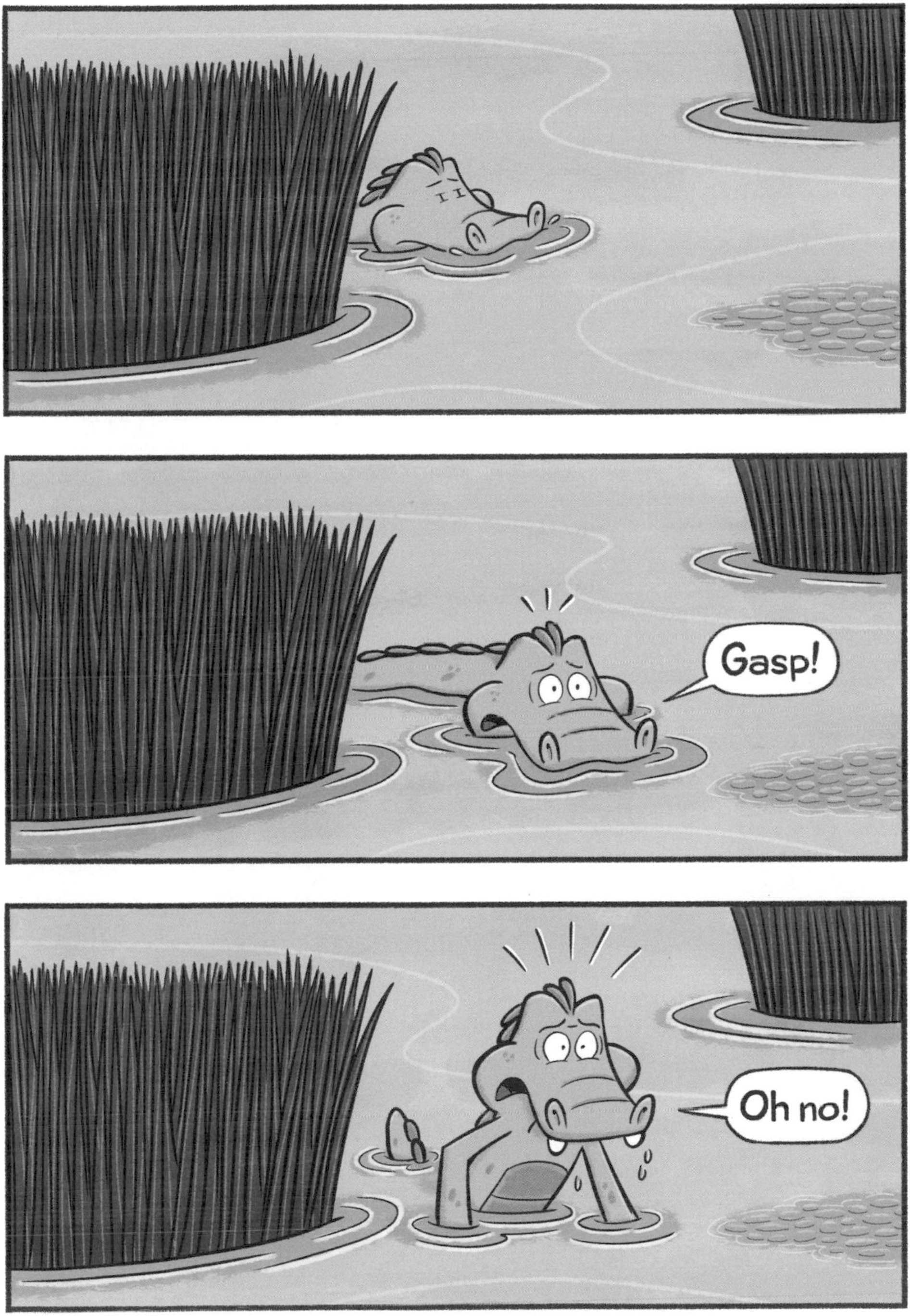
Gasp!
Oh no!

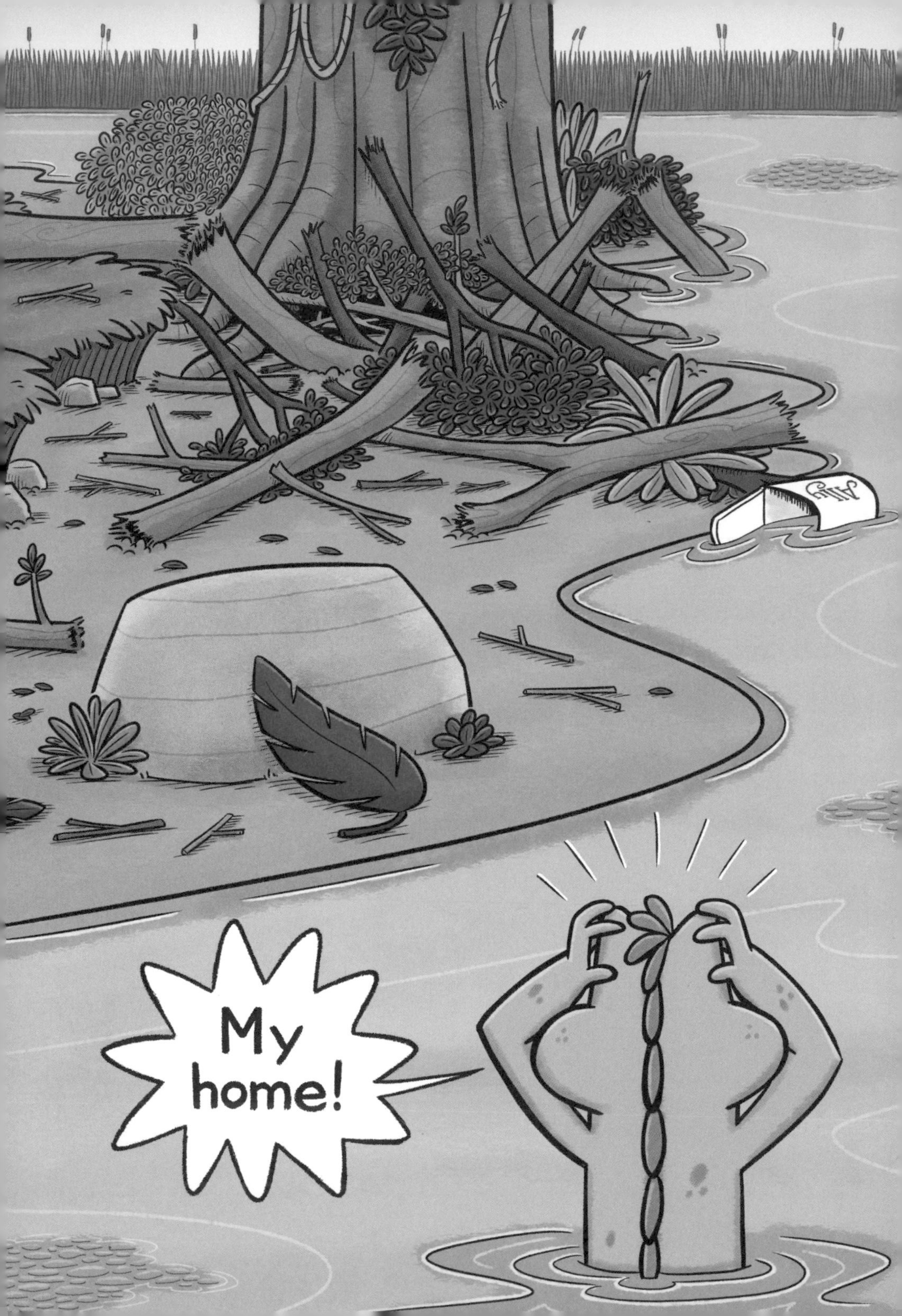
My home!

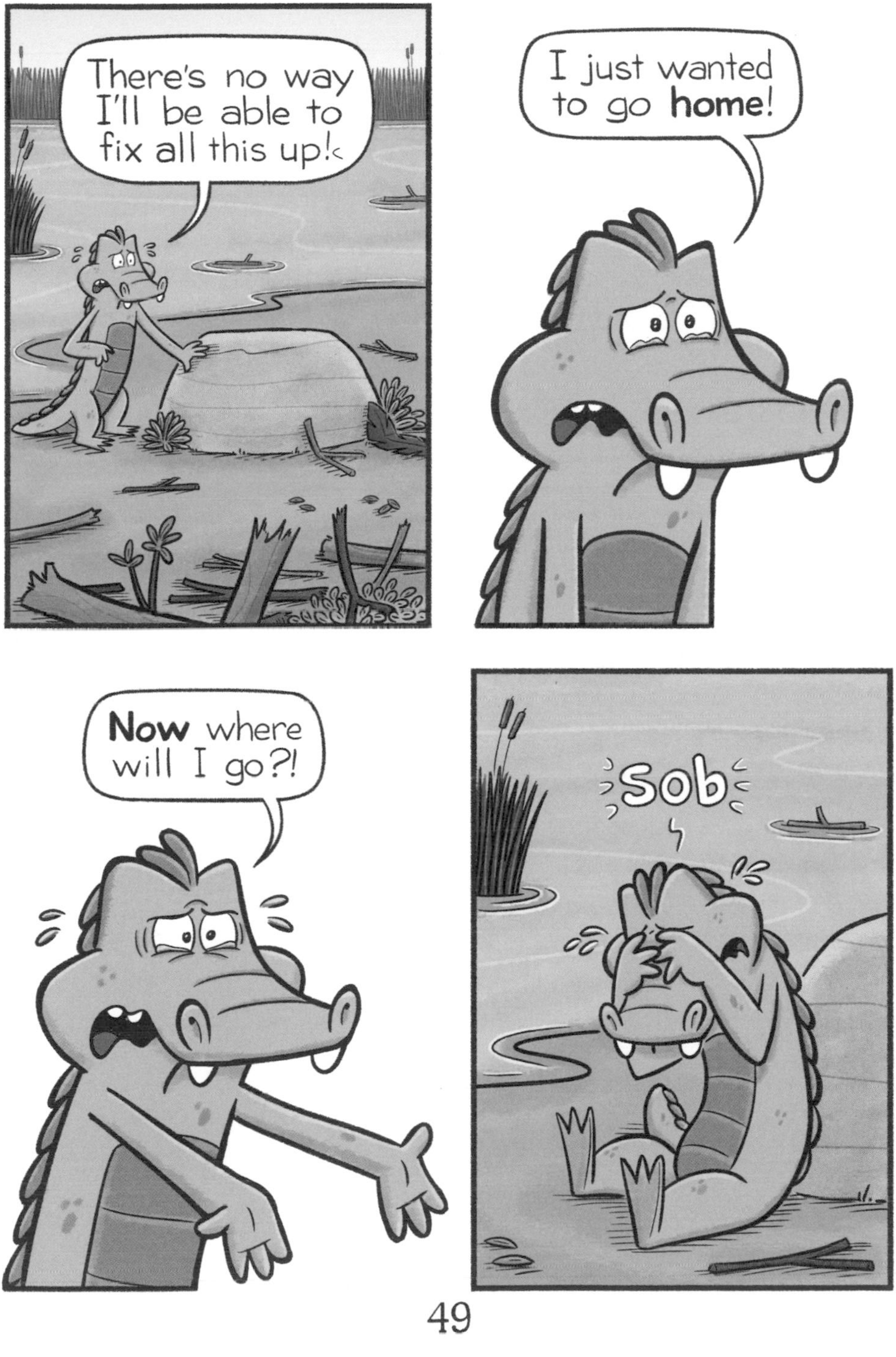
There's no way I'll be able to fix all this up!
I just wanted to go **home**!
Now where will I go?!
SOB

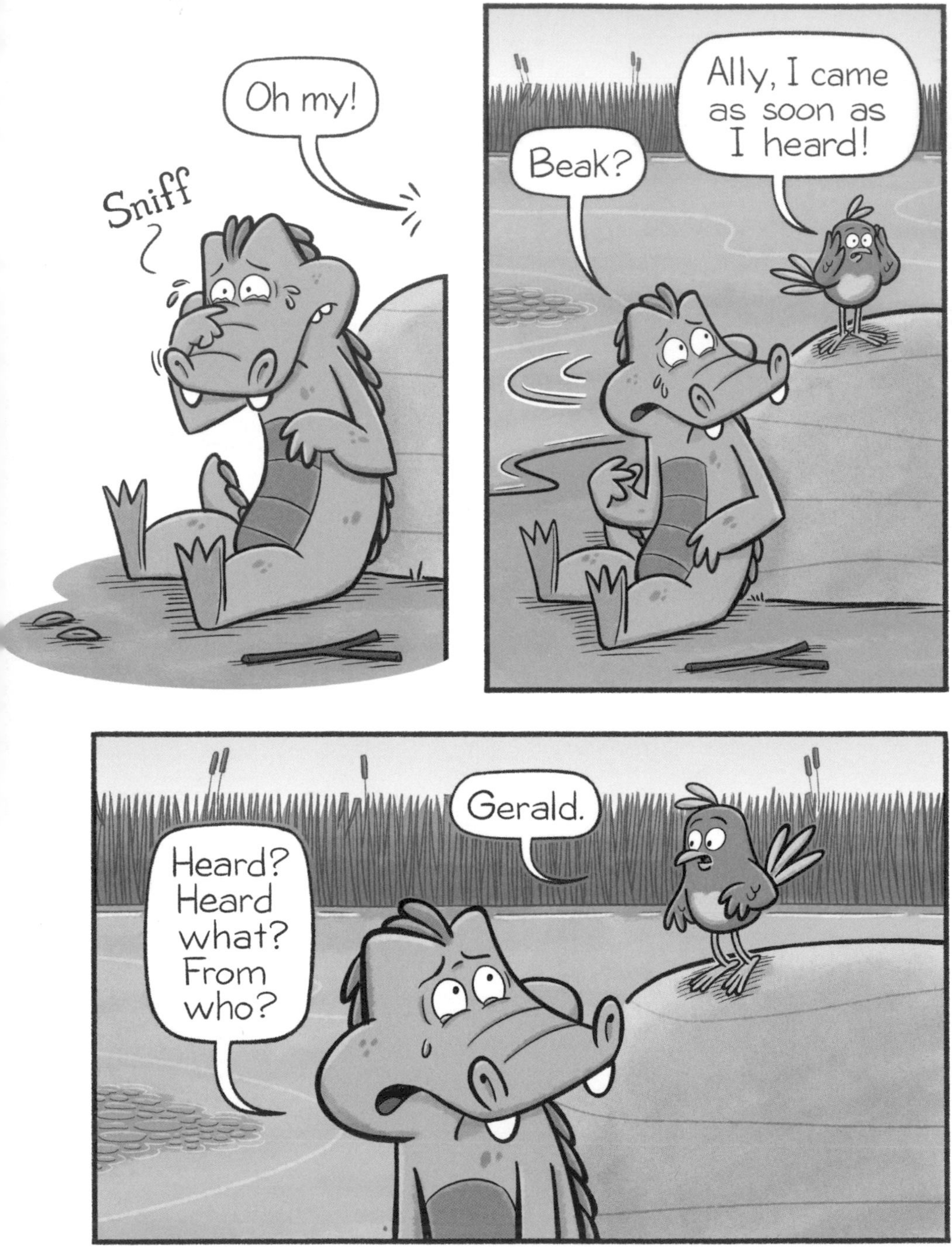
Sniff
Oh my!
Beak?
Ally, I came as soon as I heard!
Heard? Heard what? From who?
Gerald.

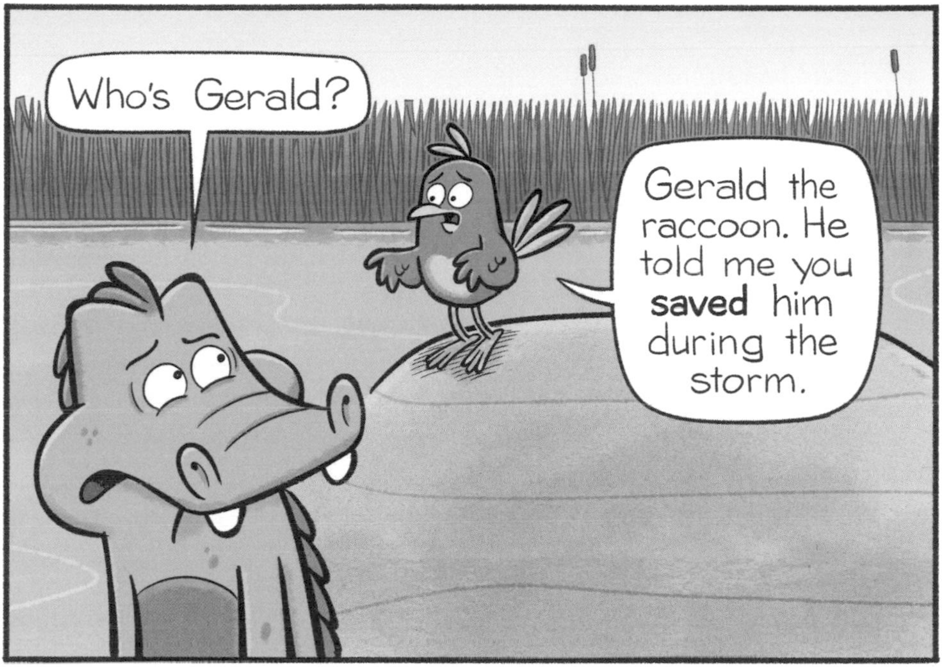
Who's Gerald?
Gerald the raccoon. He told me you **saved** him during the storm.

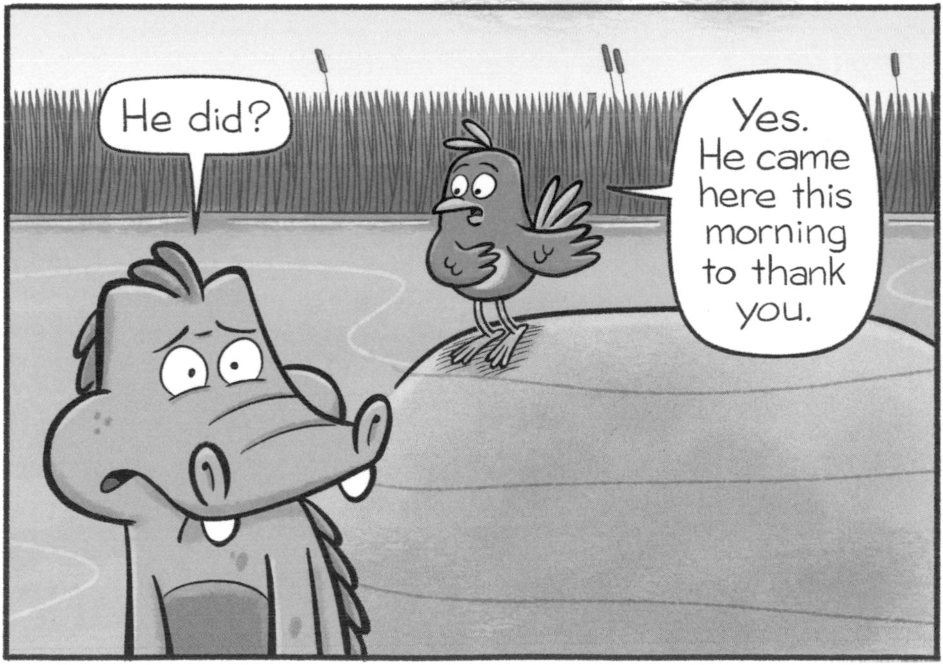
He did?
Yes. He came here this morning to thank you.

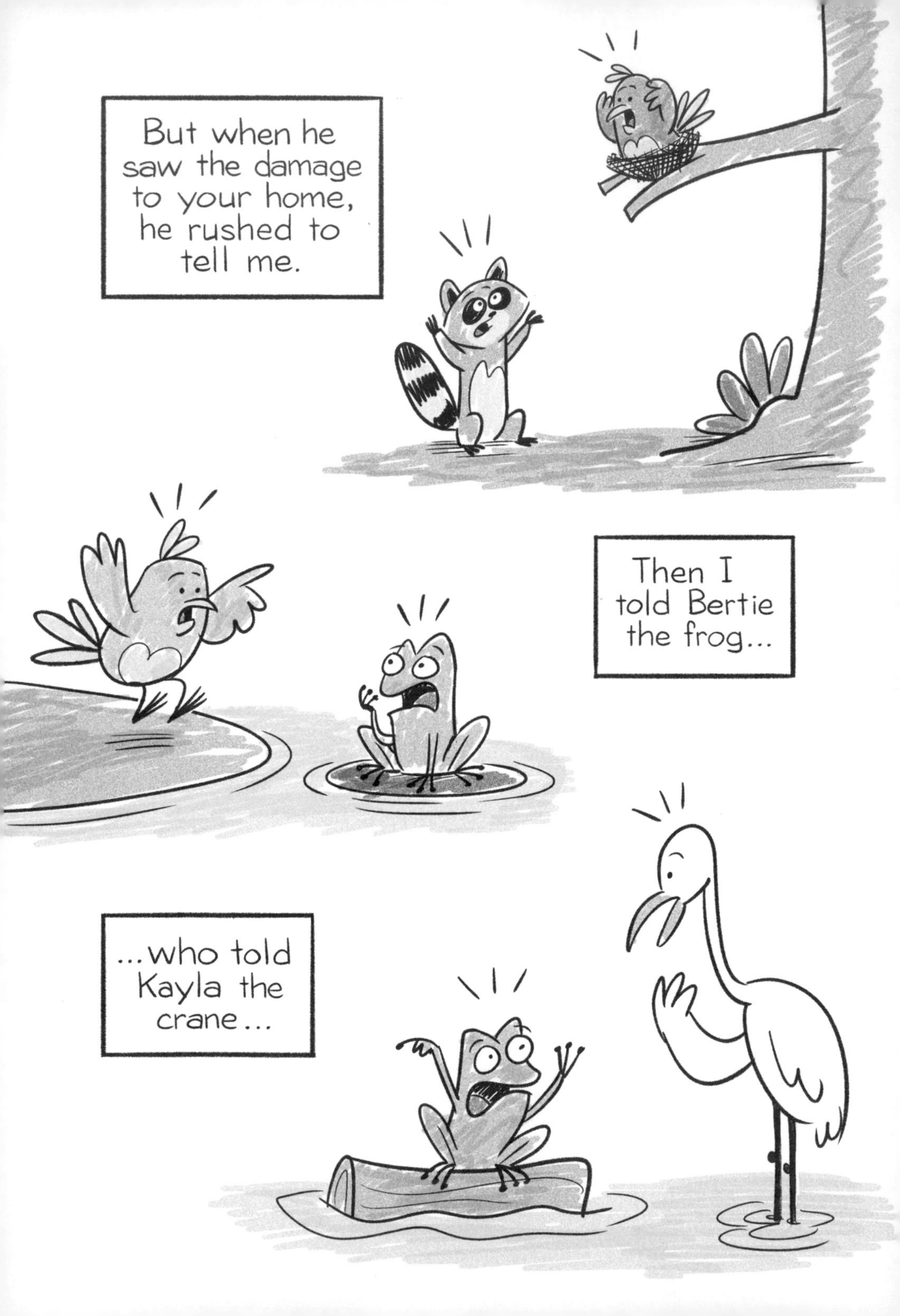

But when he saw the damage to your home, he rushed to tell me.
Then I told Bertie the frog...
...who told Kayla the crane...

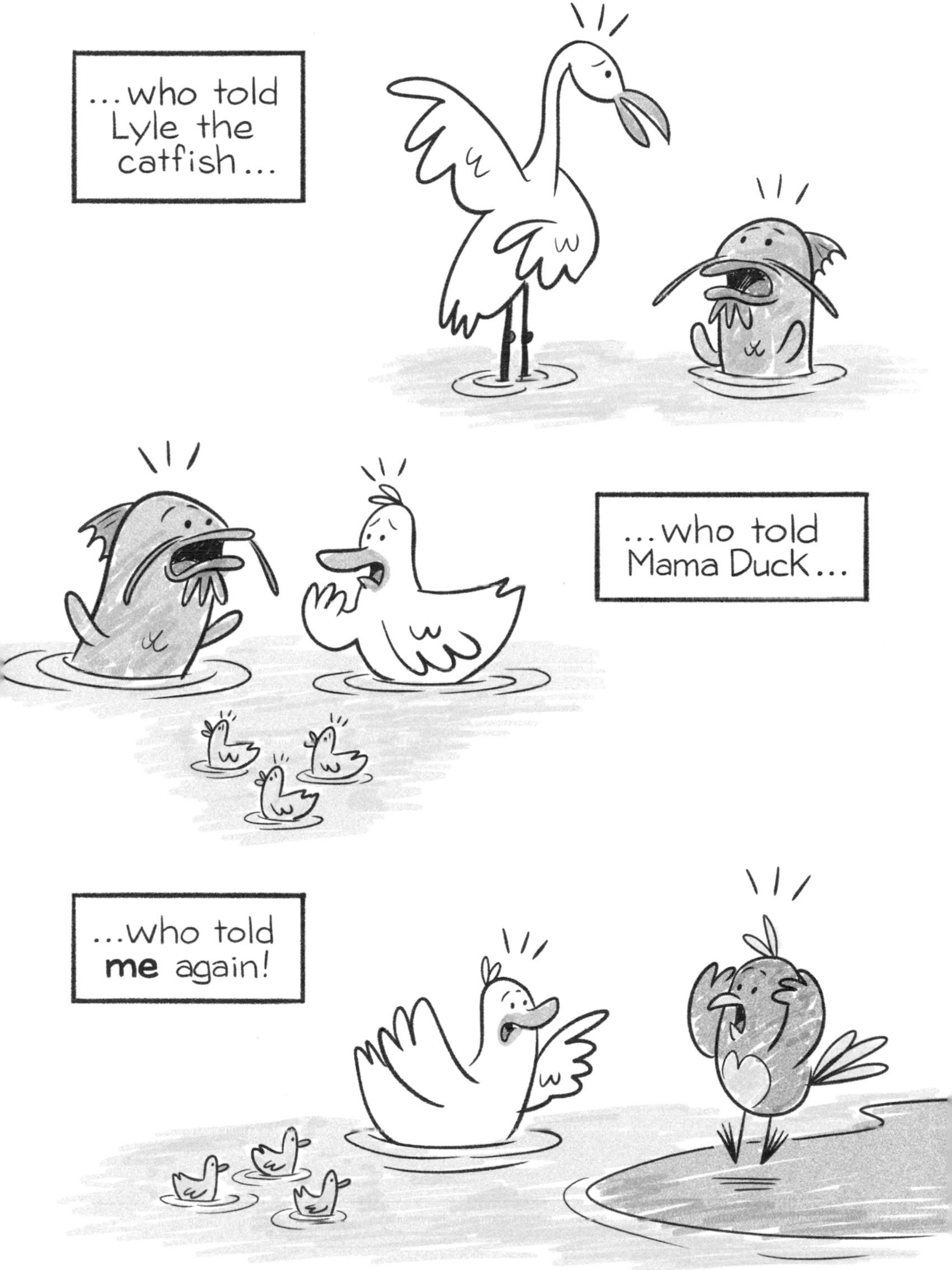
...who told Lyle the catfish...
...who told Mama Duck...
...who told **me** again!

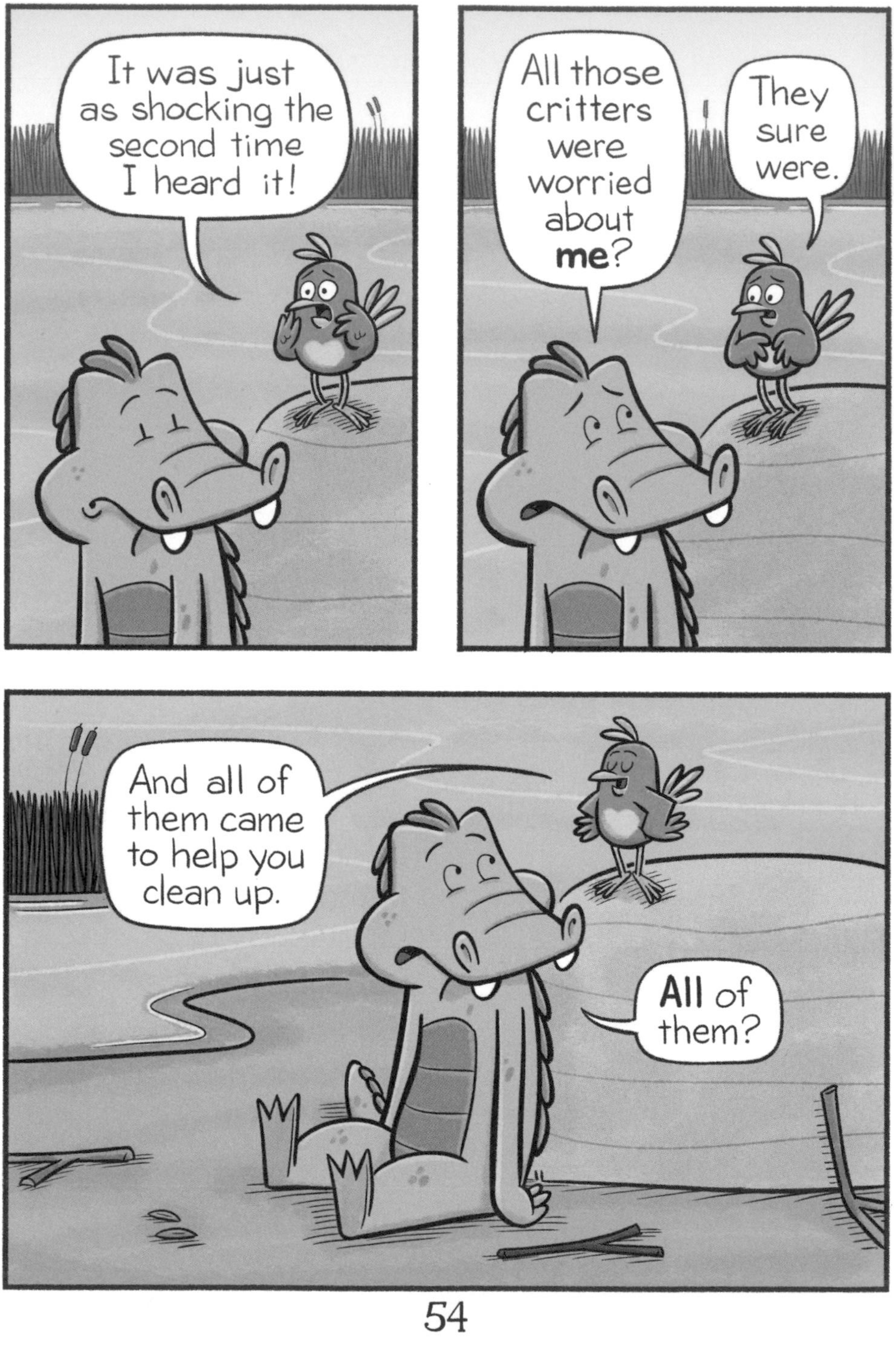
It was just as shocking the second time I heard it!
All those critters were worried about **me**?
They sure were.
And all of them came to help you clean up.
All of them?

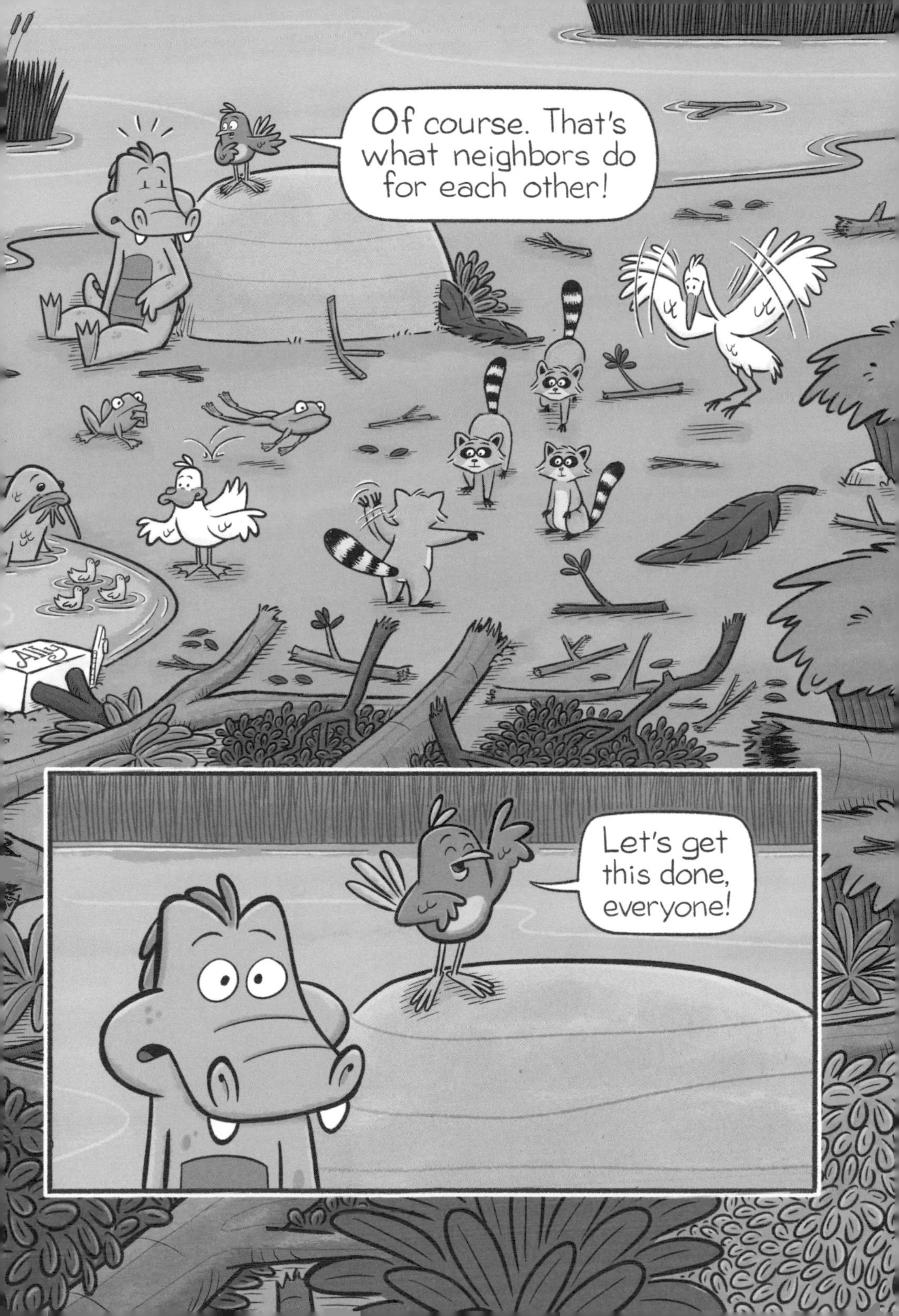
Of course. That's what neighbors do for each other!
Ally
Let's get this done, everyone!

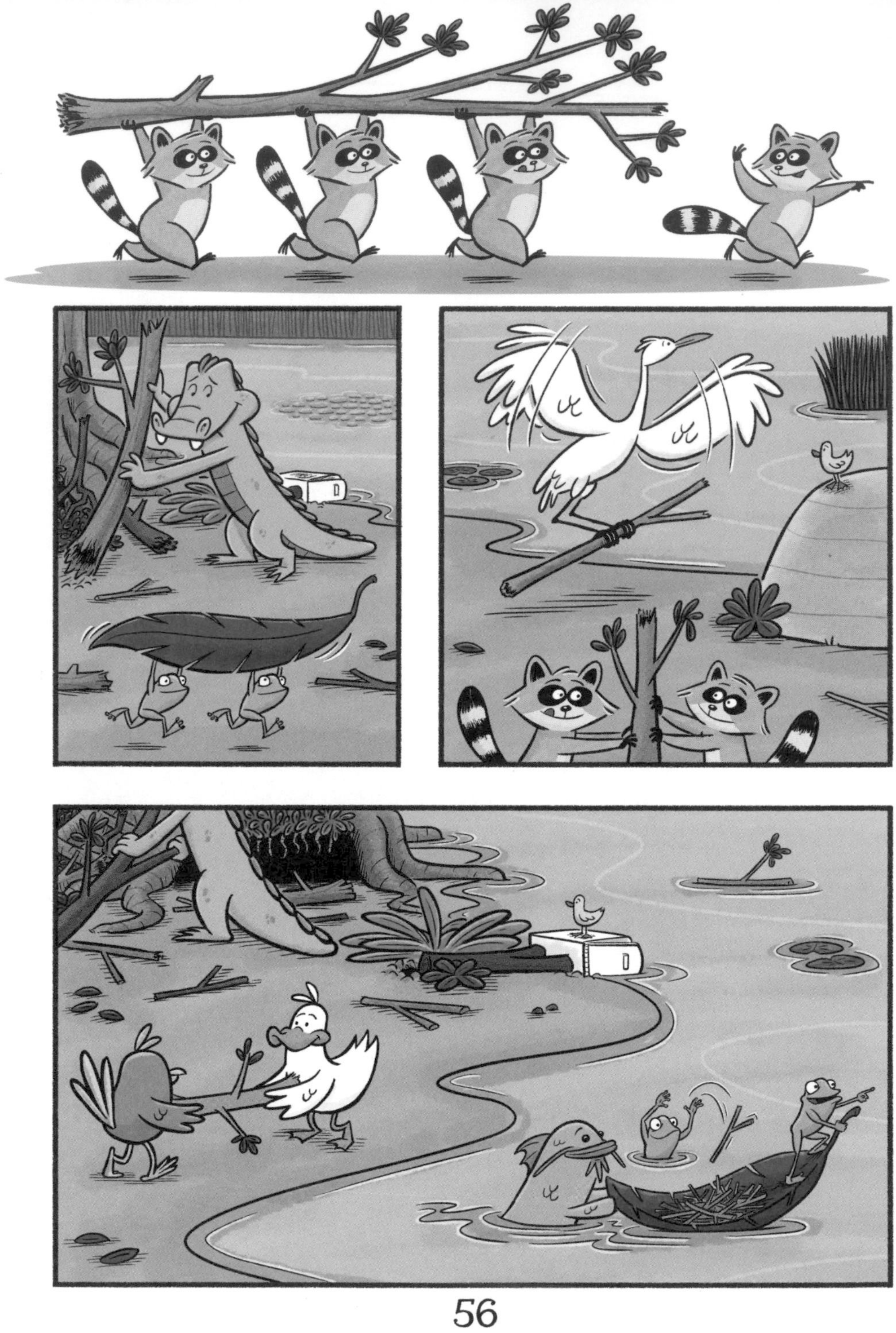

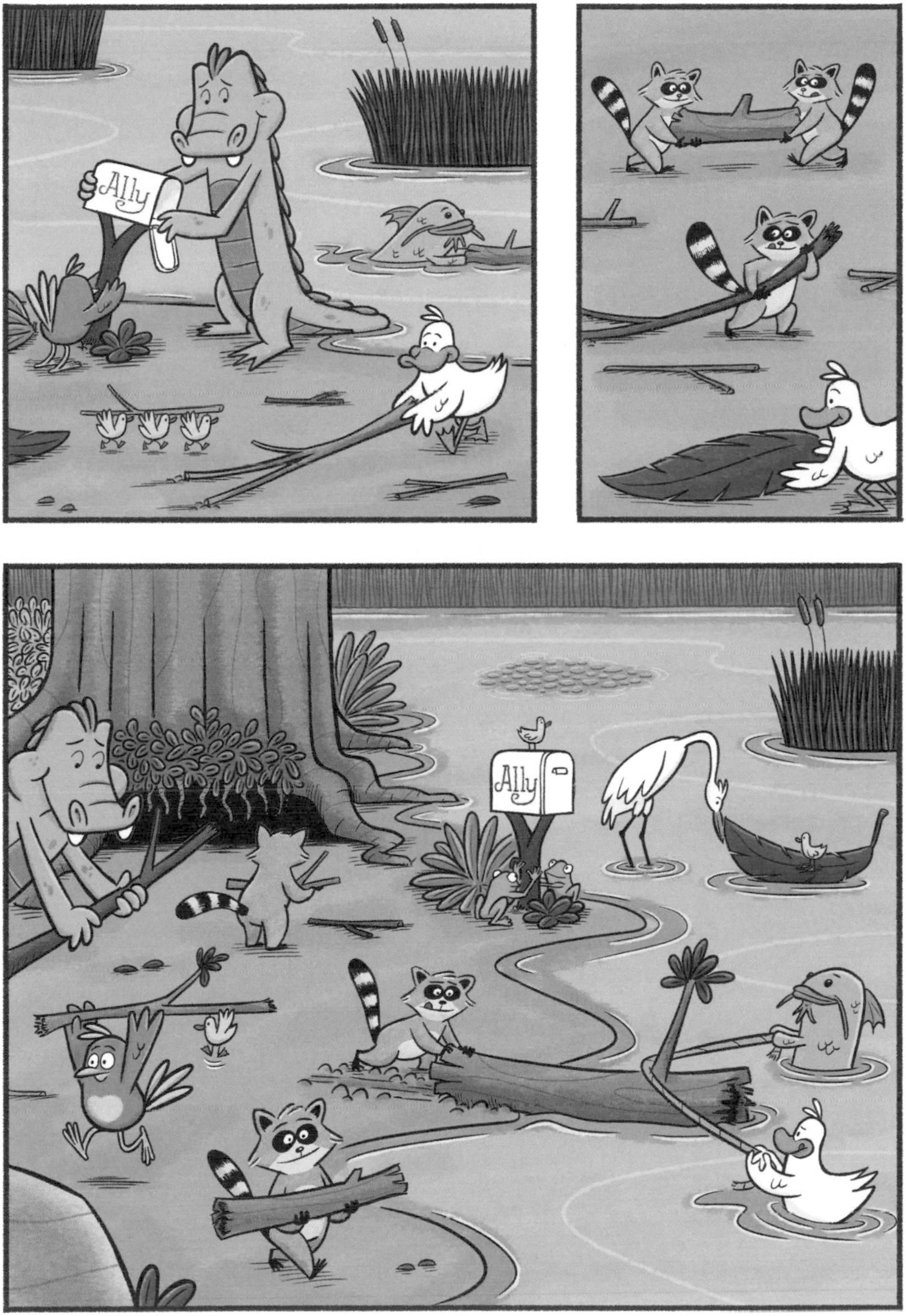
Ally
Ally

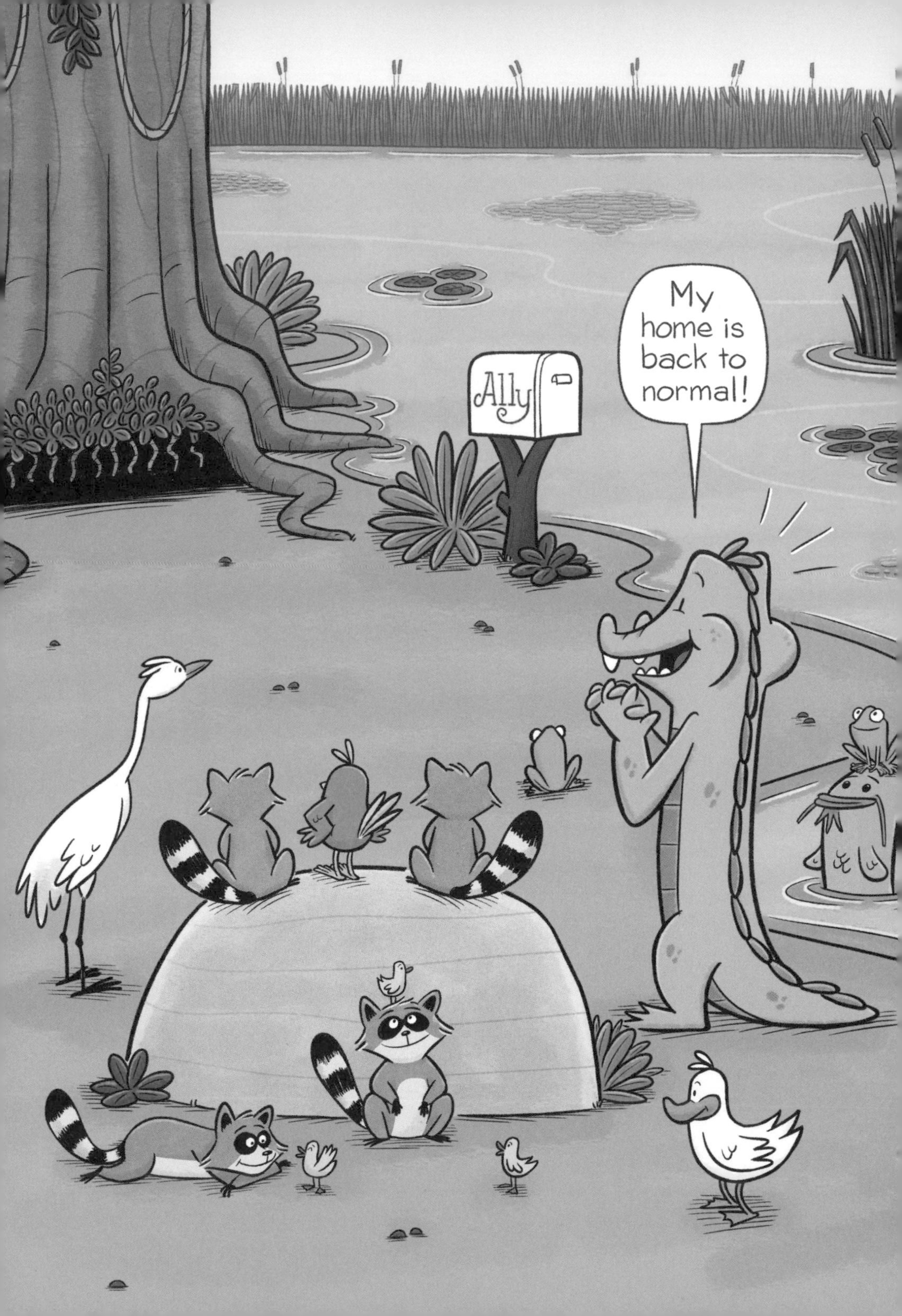
Ally
My home is back to normal!

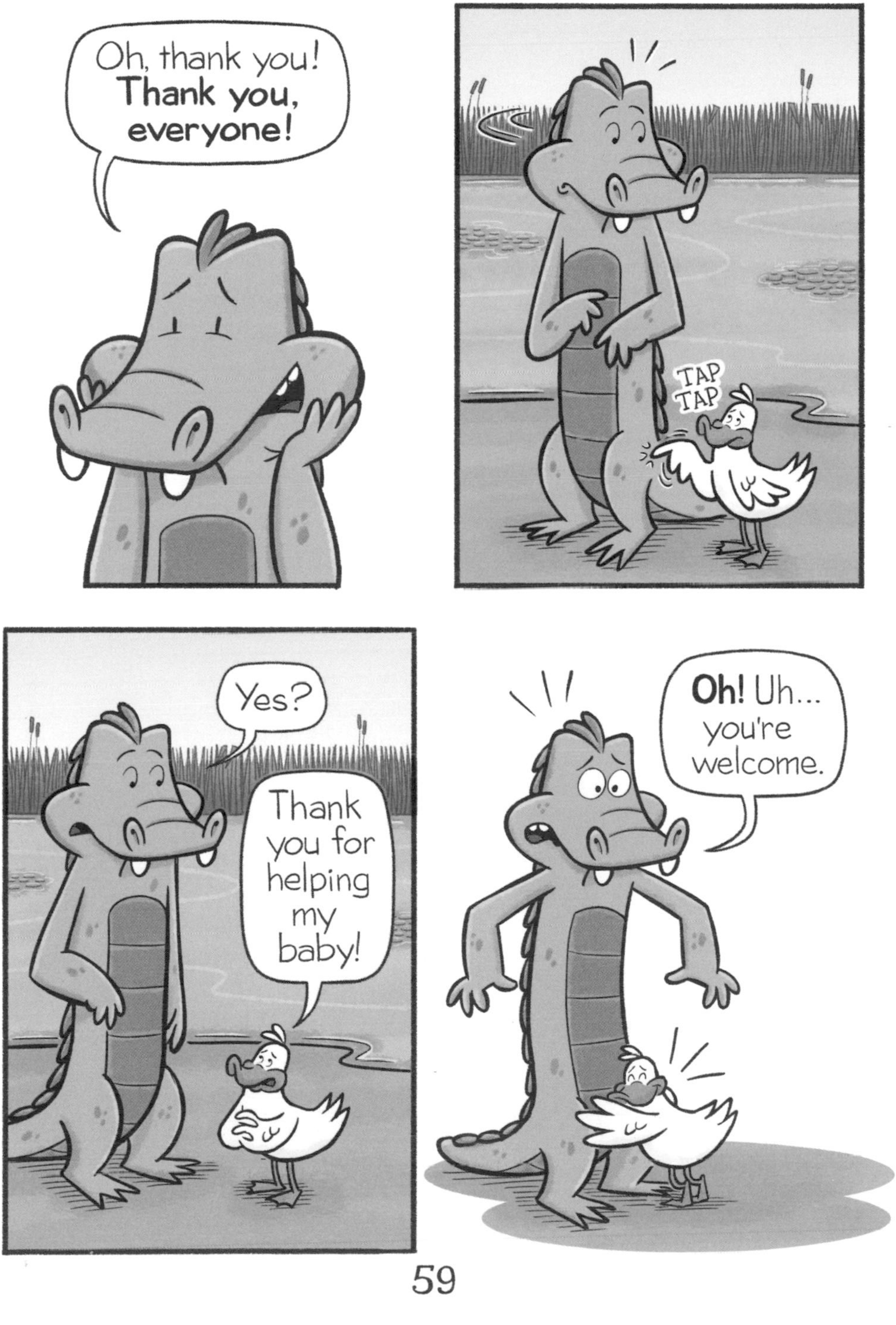
Oh, thank you! **Thank you, everyone!**
TAP TAP
Yes?
Thank you for helping my baby!
Oh! Uh... you're welcome.

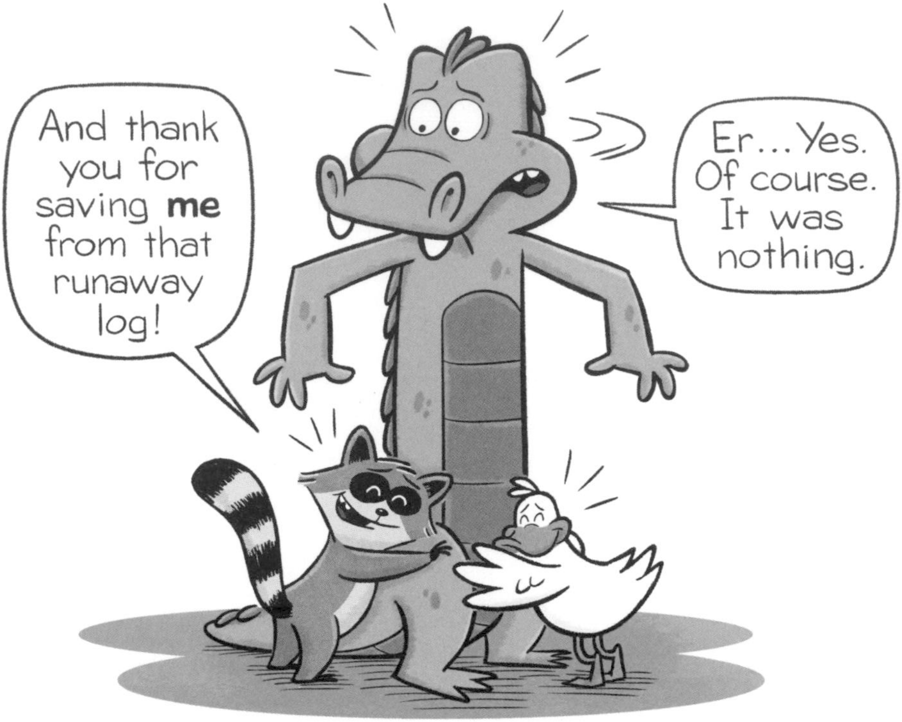
And thank you for saving **me** from that runaway log!
Er... Yes. Of course. It was nothing.

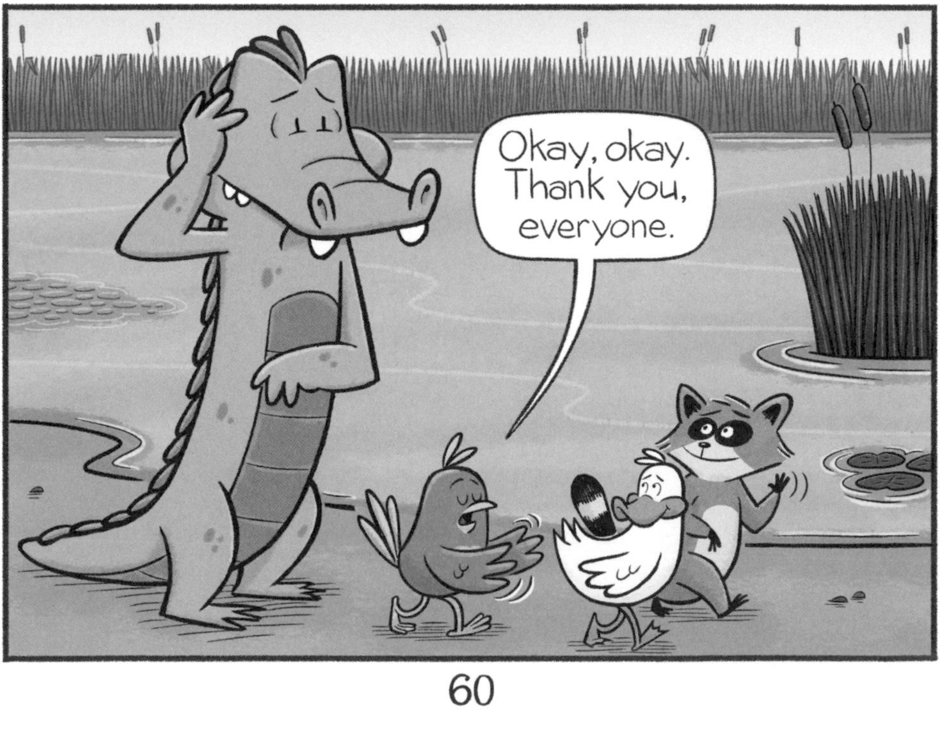
Okay, okay. Thank you, everyone.

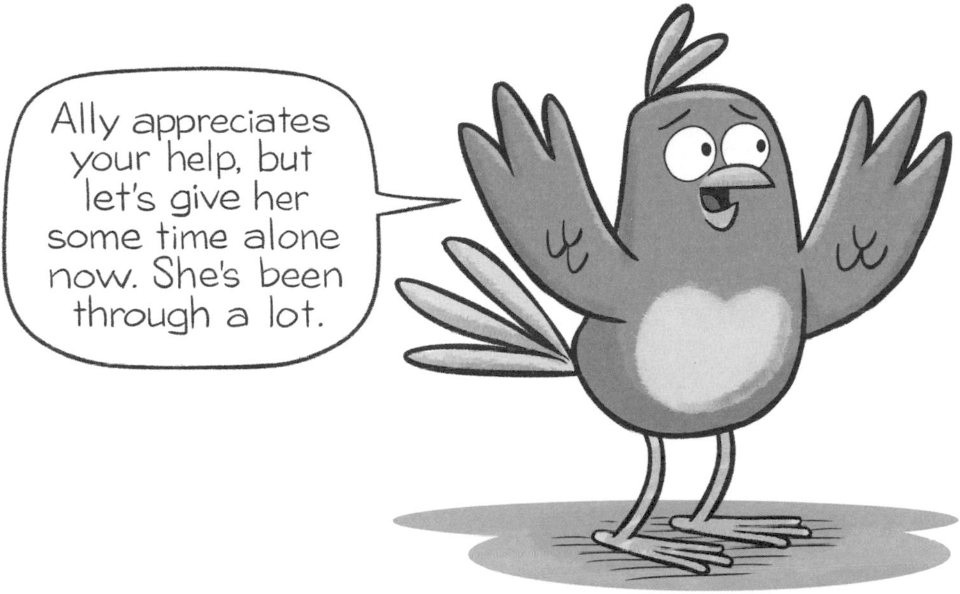
Ally appreciates your help, but let's give her some time alone now. She's been through a lot.

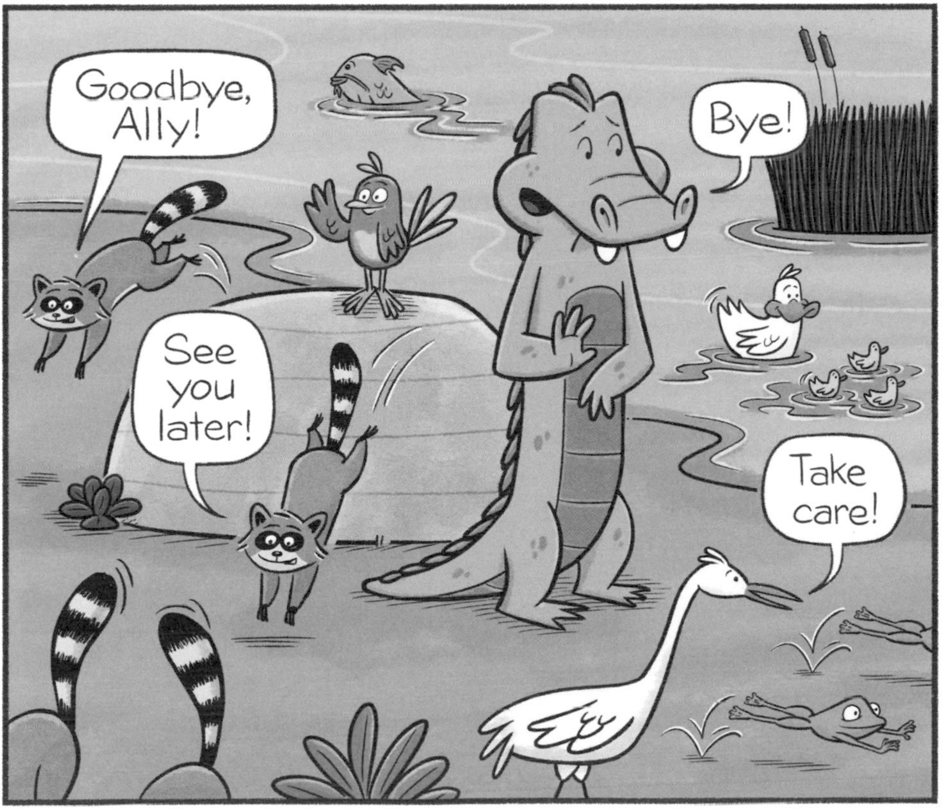
Goodbye, Ally!
Bye!
See you later!
Take care!

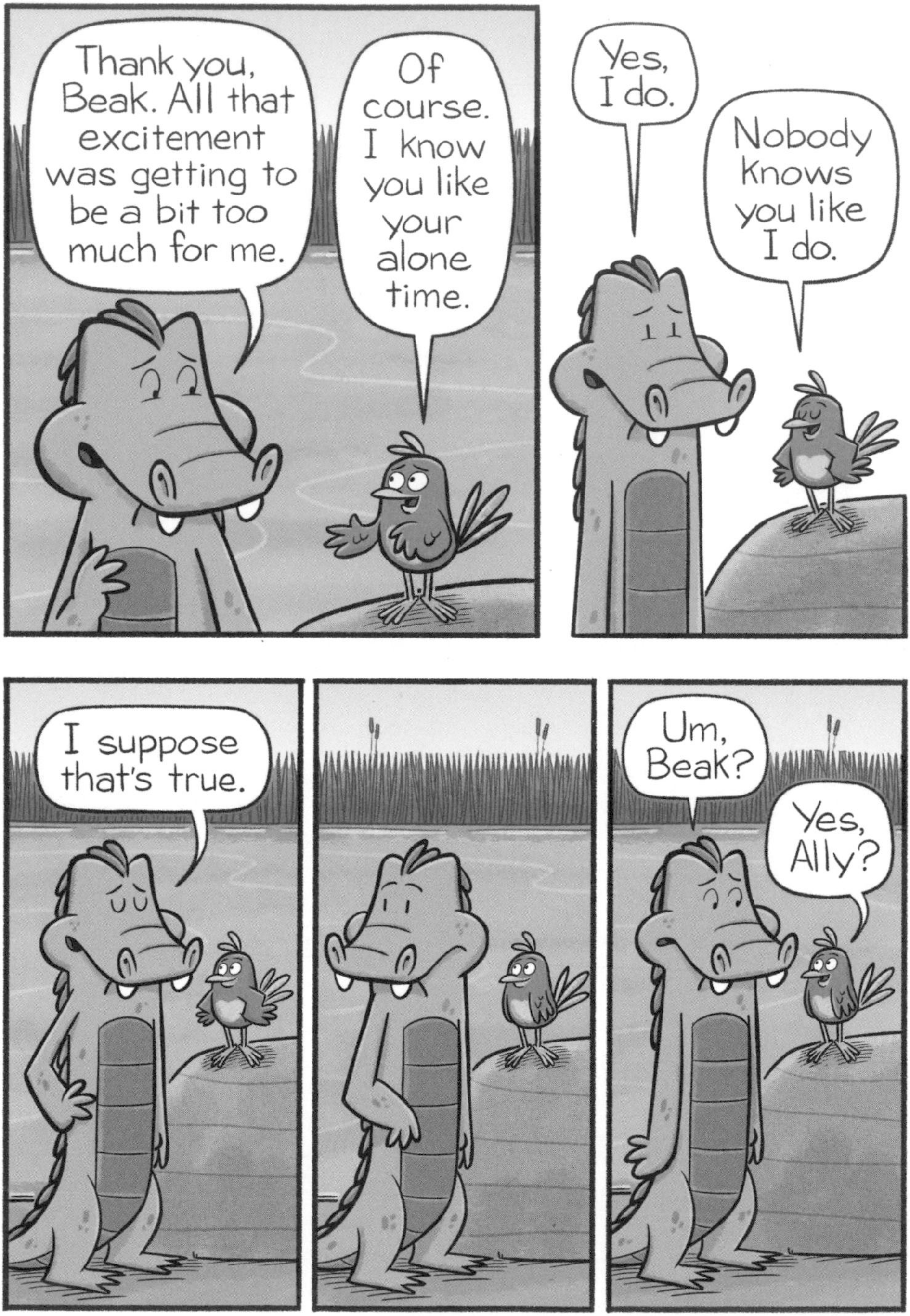
Thank you, Beak. All that excitement was getting to be a bit too much for me.
Of course. I know you like your alone time.
Yes, I do.
Nobody knows you like I do.
I suppose that's true.
Um, Beak?
Yes, Ally?

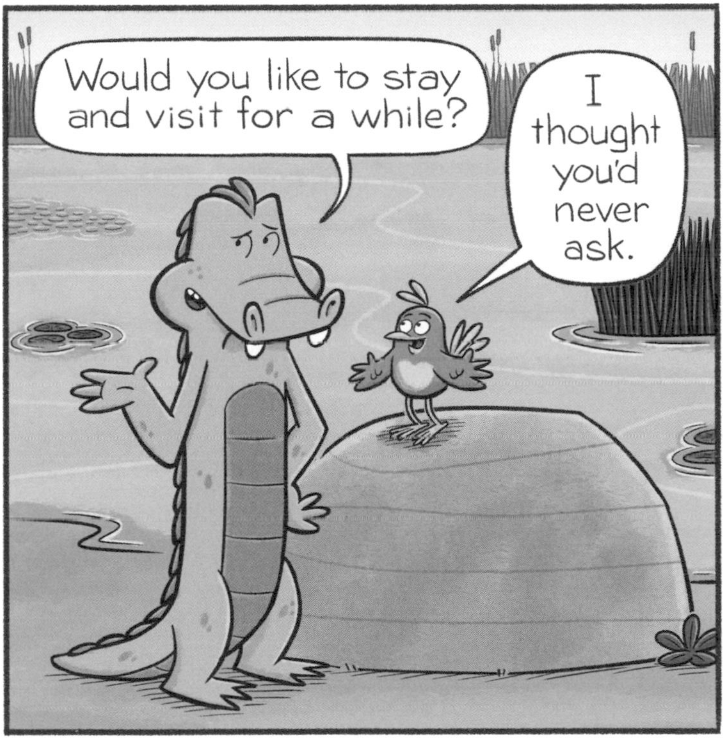
Would you like to stay and visit for a while?
I thought you'd never ask.

HarperAlley is an imprint of HarperCollins Publishers.

Beak & Ally #3: The Big Storm
Copyright © 2022 by Norm Feuti
All rights reserved. Manufactured in Bosnia and Herzegovina.
No part of this book may be used or reproduced in any manner whatsoever without
written permission except in the case of brief quotations embodied in critical
articles and reviews. For information address HarperCollins Children's Books, a
division of HarperCollins Publishers, 195 Broadway, New York, NY 10007.
www.harperalley.com

Library of Congress Control Number: 2021949298
ISBN 978-0-06-302163-1

Typography by Norm Feuti
22 23 24 25 26   GPS   10 9 8 7 6 5 4 3 2 1

First Edition

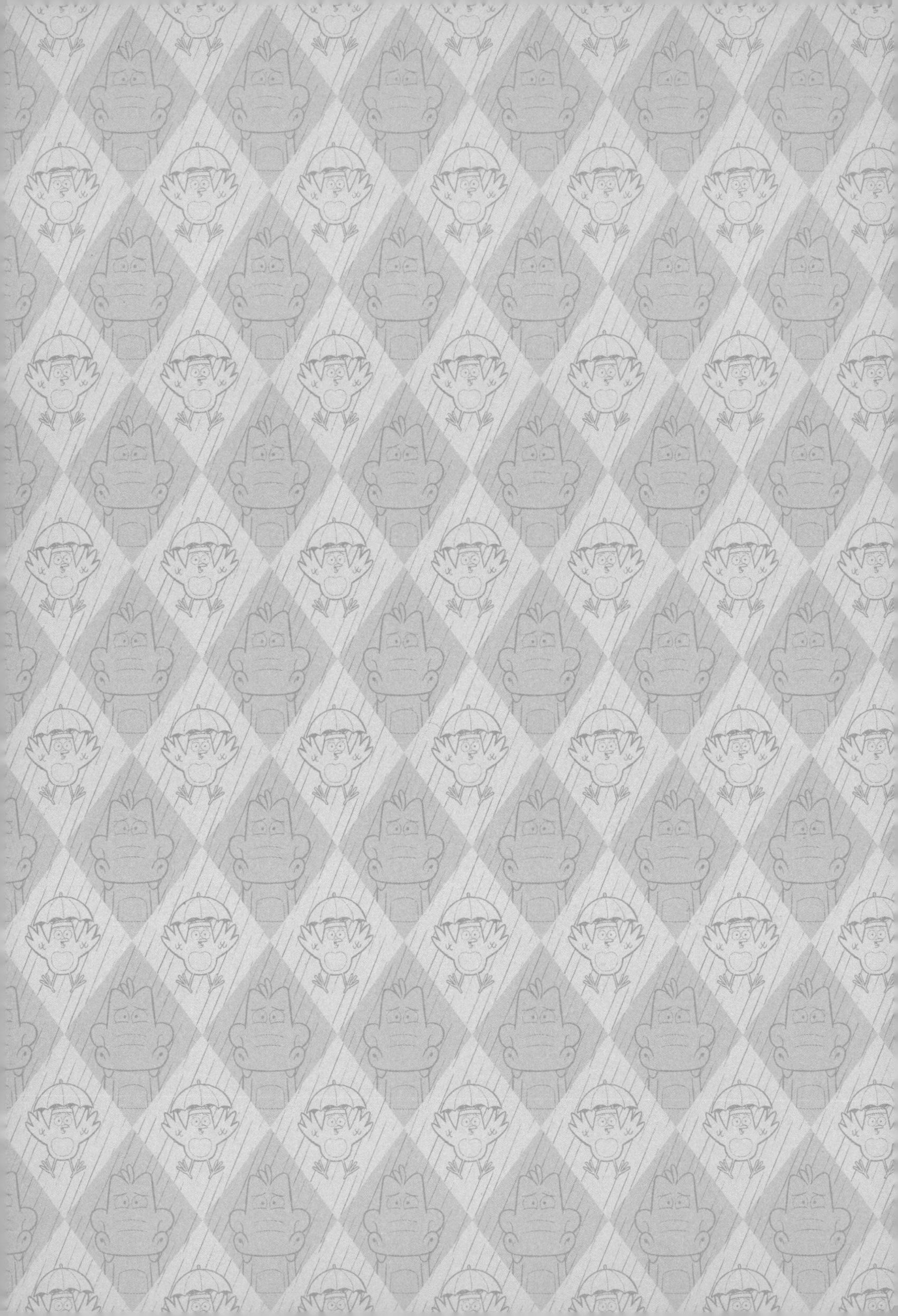